Adventures *of the* Frolic Riders

The Skeleton Creek Caper
by Annette M. Johnston

A Collaborative Publication of

Gold Leaf Press

Adventures of the Frolic Riders
The Skeleton Creek Caper
By Annette M. Johnston

Editorial Director: Rebecca J. Ensign
Cover Art: Tony Boisvert
Book and Cover Design: Boisvert Design

A Collaborative Publication of Gold Leaf Press
Detroit, MI
www.goldleafpress.com
www. frolicfarm.com

Library of Congress Control Number: 2012936553

ISBNs
Print: 10 digit: 1-886769-68-0
             13 digit: 978-1-886769-68-7
Digital: 978-1-886769-4
Available as a pdf download and formatted for all mobile devices.

128 pages; Soft cover; $14.95

1098765432

Dedication

This book is dedicated to my parents, Murray and June Johnston, who allowed me to "horse around" as a child, and also inspired a lifelong love of books and reading. I also dedicate this book to my many critter friends, including my best horse, Dajib.

Table of Contents

Adventures of the Frolic Riders
The Skeleton Creek Caper

Chapter 1
Meet the Frolic Riders

By the size of the cloud of dust that was rolling quickly toward the fort, Corporal Jordan, on look-out duty, knew they were in deep trouble. He sent up the alarm to awaken the troop, so they could spring into action. No doubt it would be a bloody battle, but all of the troop members were brave soldiers, and would not hesitate to fight. Their very lives might be at stake. Just as the Corporal was getting his weapons ready to fire, he heard a familiar voice calling to him.

"Jordan! Jeremy! It's time for dinner! Come down now!" That was Jordan's mother's voice and once he heard it, he realized he may have heard it a time or two before. This time he knew he and Jeremy better get moving. It was time to eat! He put down his slingshot.

Jordan's younger brother, Jeremy, tucked inside the "fort", which was actually a tree house, rolled up the paperback book he was reading, crammed it in his back pocket, then started climbing carefully down the rope ladder out of the tree house. Jordan followed, but slid down a long rope instead, and quickly overtook his younger brother. They raced to the back door of their house. Shoving Jeremy aside, Jordan stepped inside first. Both boys were hungry, and they smelled something good cooking in the kitchen. Sure enough, their mom had cooked one of their favorite dinners and the boys were eager to eat.

After washing off most of their "trail dirt", the boys sat down to attack the piles of food their mom had put on the table. They both reached for the pyramid of corn on the cob that was stacked on a serving dish. It was early September and fresh grown sweet corn was still in season, though not for much longer. After loading his plate, Jordan packed away two giant-sized sloppy joes, two big buttery ears of corn with plenty of salt, and a few bites of cole slaw, then washed it down with a tall glass of ice cold milk.

Mrs. Chambers watched all this in amazement; she couldn't understand how a boy who could eat like that could stay so skinny. As Jordan took his last gulp of milk, the only thing left from the mound of food that was on his plate just a few minutes earlier was the kernels of corn that were dangling on his chin. "Wipe your face, Jordan," Mrs. Chambers said as her eyes glanced to ten year old Jeremy, who enjoyed the dinner, but ate more carefully.

Jeremy was neat and studious, and his eating habits followed suit. He would take a bite of sloppy joe, then look around, pinch off a couple smaller bites and sneak them to their dog, Laddie, who knew right where to wait. Jeremy continued this routine until he – and Laddie – had polished off two sloppy joes.

As Jordan wadded up his napkin and Jeremy folded his, the two boys started their usual negotiations over who was supposed to clear the table and who would load the dishwasher. The winner of this discussion was the one who got to load the dishwasher; tonight, the winner was Jordan. Once the kitchen work was done, the boys dove into their homework. Now most kids would drag this part of the night out as long as they could, but not Jeremy and Jordan; kitchen chores and homework were their ticket to the best part of the day – going out to the barn to let their horses in from the pasture and taking them for a ride.

Jordan's horse was a beautiful bay gelding named Banner. He looked eager for a nice ride, and waited impatiently by the gate to be let in for grooming and saddling. Banner was a sturdily-built horse, very well-trained, and at 12 was a year older than Jordan. Jeremy was convinced there was something very special about Banner. And, even though he didn't get to ride him, he liked to bring him treats and pet him.

Jeremy's horse was a small, pretty chestnut mare named Penny. Penny was a little younger than Banner; she was cat-like and quick, and had a long, flaxen mane and tail that was just about the same shade as both boys' blond hair. Like Banner, Penny loved her young master too, and was very willing to please. She especially liked the carrots that Jeremy brought her.

To get ready to ride, the boys quickly groomed both horses as their mother had taught them, and then saddled them with their big western saddles and colorful saddle pads. They put on their bright orange-colored helmets (their mom insisted), swung into their saddles, and rode off down their quiet country lane to see what fun they could dream up. They jogged slowly down the edge of their pasture, and then took a well-worn path through the woods. The horses walked carefully through the woods, jumping over fallen tree branches across the trail and under overhanging branches which made Jordan and Jeremy have to duck once in a while to avoid being hit by them. When he was younger, Jordan liked to let the branches snap back into Jeremy's face, but after Jeremy got cut right above his eye, Jordan realized that was more dangerous than funny.

They soon came to a wooden bridge over Skeleton Creek, a narrow, winding creek that looked deeper than it actually was. Both horses began to cross it barely even looking at the water. As they reached the midpoint, Jeremy said, "Remember when Banner used to fuss about going over this bridge? I always thought it was because he was scared of the name. He crosses perfect now."

Jordan snorted, "Yeah, like he really knew the creek was named Skeleton Creek. He's a horse, not a person, you know."

Jeremy spoke up quickly. "I know. But he's a really smart horse."

As they neared the other side of the bridge, neither boy noticed a shiny metal object at the bottom of the creek, but Banner took a good look at it without breaking stride.

The boys rode on quietly, with just the sound of the hoof beats, and the creaking of the leather saddles. Soon they arrived at their friend Chip's house, where he lived with his parents and his eight year old sister, Molly. Chip's family's farm was small, like the Chambers' farm, but it wasn't kept up as well. Chip's dad was a truck driver so he was only home six or seven days a month, which explained why the house and barn didn't get painted and the fences leaned sideways. After each thunderstorm, Jeremy and Jordan were always glad when they saw that the fences hadn't collapsed.

Chip Easton was in Jordan's 6th grade class, and they were best friends. Chip was a stocky boy, with sparkling brown eyes and dark hair that always looked uncombed. Chip already had his horse, Rocket, saddled and ready to go when Jordan and Jeremy arrived. He quickly tied up his dog, Jake, so he wouldn't follow them. Rocket was a fast horse, dark brown in color, with a short black mane and a long black tail that he liked to swish impatiently when Chip held him back.

"Put on your helmet," Chip's mom called out to Chip as he and Rocket began riding off toward Chip's corral. Chip put on his helmet, which was pretty banged up but useable, as they reached the corral for riding practice. They all needed to improve their form if they were going to do well at the Frolic Riders meeting the next day.

They worked on a slow jog first, then on cantering.

"You look like a chicken," Jordan told Jeremy. "Stop flapping your elbows like that."

"I'm not working on my elbows right now. I'm working on keeping my heels down," Jeremy said as his arms flapped even more.

Jordan replied, "Better work on those elbows too!"

After just a few minutes, Chip yelled, "Aw, heck with this, let's ride!"

All three boys broke out in a brisk ride around the pasture. On the smoothest part, they let the horses race, which was where Rocket shined. He sped in front of Banner and Penny, and won easily, as usual. To cool down the horses, the boys slowed them to a walk for several minutes. Suddenly, they heard the clippity clop of a small black pony coming fast toward them. Molly was riding furiously as she approached the boys.

Although Chip loved his sister, he felt she was a pest most of the time. Molly was a dark-haired, spunky girl, who tried to keep up with her big brother and his friends, and was usually successful. Jordan tolerated her, but Jeremy actually liked Molly and they were good friends.

"You could have waited for me," Molly fumed as she rode up to the boys and their horses. "I had to finish the dishes."

Chip replied, "We don't want you here, Molly. This is for guys only, not little girls. You can't keep up."

"I can so!" Molly piped up. "Midnight can run fast. He's just short."

Jordan, the peacemaker, calmed them both down and distracted them with a suggestion to canter down the grassy lane leading back toward the corral. All four took off, with Rocket in the lead and Midnight trailing behind. At the end of the lane, they stopped to let the horses rest a bit. Then, Jordan and Jeremy said their goodbyes; it was getting dark and time for them to head for home. They rode back slowly to cool their horses down, as they had been taught.

"Think we're getting any better with our riding?" Jeremy asked Jordan. "I'd like to do well at our meeting tomorrow night."

"Well, I'll put it this way – one of us is getting better," Jordan replied.

Jeremy just shrugged as they both rode toward the barn. They quickly unsaddled their horses, put them in their stalls, and fed them hay. Mrs. Chambers came out to double check that the horses were cool enough for their grain and water. Satisfied, she let the boys finish feeding Banner and Penny and went back in the house.

Once their barn chores were done, the boys went inside the house. Since there was nothing on TV that they were allowed to watch, Jordan headed straight for the computer to play games, while Jeremy started practicing the piano. Jordan didn't understand why his brother preferred to play the piano instead of computer and video games, but he was glad he did – computer time was one thing they never argued about. Jordan got it all to himself.

Before they knew it, it was time for bed. After putting on their pajamas and climbing into bed, Jordan yelled out from his bedroom, "Mom, can we read for a few minutes before we go to sleep?"

"Just for a few minutes," Mrs. Chambers said as she approached Jordan's door. Jordan grabbed a comic book from under his bed while Jeremy pulled out the book he was reading, which was still stuffed in the back pocket of the pants he had worn that day.

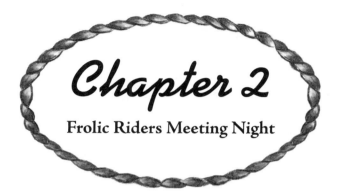

Chapter 2
Frolic Riders Meeting Night

The next day, after the boys came home from school, they finished their homework, and rushed through an early dinner. Tonight was the first Frolic Riders meeting of the fall. Jordan and Jeremy quickly groomed Penny and Banner then loaded all the necessary tack along with their horses into the horse trailer that was hooked up to their SUV. Mrs. Chambers was waiting in the driver's seat.

"Let's go boys, or else we'll be late," Mrs. Chambers yelled as the boys scrambled to get in the car and buckle their seatbelts.

"What's this?" Jordan asked as he lifted himself up from the seat.

"You're sitting on my laptop, Jordan. I'm going to catch up on some work during the meeting. Just put it in between you and Jeremy and it won't bother you." Then, they were off.

In Frolicville, Michigan, and the other small towns in the part of Michigan where the boys lived, many of the kids lived on farms or homes with a few acres of land. So, just about every kid either had a horse or at least knew how to ride, and many of them joined Riders clubs. Frolicville was home to the Frolic Riders Club, and Jordan, Jeremy, Chip, and Molly were proud to be members.

During the fall, spring and summer, they had a meeting once a week with their horses. In the winter months, they only had one monthly meeting with horses. The other meetings were mostly horsemanship classes and quiz games.

But, regardless of the time of year, with or without horses, all Riders enjoyed the meetings; this was especially true for Jordan, Jeremy, Chip, and Molly. This was because, even though they were called meetings, only a few minutes at the beginning was spent lecturing on things like care and feeding of their horses and of course, safety. The boys found this part a bit dull, but managed to pay pretty good attention since they knew they would learn how to take better care of their horses.

After the lecture part, announcements were made about upcoming events, such as trail rides, game nights, horse shows, parades and camping trips, which they all participated in. The rest of the meeting was spent practicing horsemanship.

Like all Riders Clubs, Frolic Riders were divided into age and skill level groups and competed in horse shows and other exciting events. Molly, in 3rd grade, was a Cadet, the beginner group for kids in 1st - 3rd grade. Jeremy, Jordan and Chip joined the Riders club three years ago, and started out as Cadets; but now they were Junior Riders, who were kids in 4th - 8th grade. They couldn't wait until they were old enough to be Senior Riders, who were high school kids. And they all had their eyes on becoming Elite Riders, which were the troop leaders and best horsemen.

But, until a Rider became an Elite Rider, he or she could earn badges by showing ability in various skills like how to properly lead, groom, saddle, bridle, mount, dismount, and control a horse at a walk, trot, and canter; they could also earn a badge for knowing proper safety techniques. Jordan, Jeremy and Chip had earned several of these badges and wore them proudly on their troop uniforms.

The meeting on this night was with the full troop. There were 10 Cadets, 15 Juniors, 16 Senior Riders, 4 Elites and four parents who helped the Elites lead the meeting. Usually there were five leader parents at a meeting, but the kids found out, mostly through whispers, that one of the leader parents had his car stolen that day and had to meet with the police.

After the Riders and their horses were unloaded and tacked up, Amanda Morgan, an Elite Rider and definitely the most popular girl in the troop, asked for everyone's attention.

"Welcome everyone, to our first fall meeting. Tonight's meeting will be partly devoted to riding techniques, and then we have a special guest – Cowboy Bill, who will give a roping demonstration." Amanda looked around to make sure everyone was listening, then continued. "Afterwards, he'll help you try it yourselves."

"Cool!" Chip said while fumbling through his saddle bag to make sure he had a rope with him. "I can't wait to shake out a loop."

Jordan and Jeremy both cracked up as Chip wiggled his hips like he was hula-hooping while trying to mount Rocket. After a bit of a struggle, Chip was secure in Rocket's saddle and all three boys rode to join their group.

The Junior Riders rode their horses around the arena as various commands were given. Chip had some trouble with Rocket, who was a little too energetic with his canter and his trot. "Slow down, boy," Chip said as Rocket sped past the other horses.

The boys and their horses responded to each command, trying to execute perfectly. All in all, they did fairly well, but needed more work; Jeremy needed to work on his elbows; Jordan had to practice keeping his heels down and Chip, well, Chip had to work on both his heels and his elbows, and "slow your horse down," Mr. Grimmer, one of the leader parents, told him.

Molly rode Midnight with the other Cadets in the smaller corral, and the two did very well. Midnight was one of the few ponies that actually behaved properly, unlike most of the other ponies that pretty much did what they wanted.

The troop then gathered back in the arena and enjoyed watching Cowboy Bill - a real cowboy - give a roping demonstration. Cowboy Bill showed them how to shake out a loop, whirl it around over his head, and rope a dummy calf. Jordan, Jeremy, and Chip watched carefully and then jumped out of their seats when it was time to try it. Jordan had a hard time, and never quite managed to get his rope over the calf's head. Jeremy was patient and did a little better. After five tries, he managed to get his lariat over the calf's head and horns, and jerked it tight.

After whirling the rope around his head about ten times, Chip extended his arm and accidentally roped Cowboy Bill, who was standing too close to the dummy calf. Jordan and Jeremy held back their laughter as red-faced Chip apologized to Cowboy Bill. Some of the other kids howled with laughter.

Untangling himself, Cowboy Bill said, "That's OK, son. You've got a heckuva arm, you just need to work on your aim."

After the troop meeting, the three boys unsaddled their horses, properly making sure they were securely tied to the trailers, and then walked over to the rail to watch the drill team perform some exciting drill team movements. They stared in amazement as the drill team did some scary looking things. Starting in groups four abreast, they cantered around the arena, split into single file going in opposite directions, then crossed directly in front of each other in a serpentine movement.

"Geez, that is awesome! We can't even ride in pairs at a walk when we're in a parade, look what they can do!" Jordan said rather loudly.

"We'll get the hang of it," Jeremy said, "We just need to practice some more."

"Yeah, I 'spose," Jordan said as the drill team wrapped up their practice session. Across the arena, in the pasture, the Elite Riders started up a game of broom polo and invited a few of the Senior Riders to join them.

"I wish we could play," Chip complained.

"We will someday, when our uniforms and sashes are plastered with as many badges as they have," Jordan said.

"Yeah, well, I still wish they'd let us play," Chip complained. "Rocket would be really good at broom polo, he's so fast."

"So would Banner, that is, if Mom would let Banner play." Jordan added.

Just then, Molly walked up to the boys and said, "Look, you guys, I just got another badge. I've done all the tests right with Midnight, and I'm going to be a Junior Rider too, real soon!"

"Not so fast, Molly," cautioned Jeremy. "You have to be in 4th grade to make Junior Rider. I thought you knew that."

"Well, I will be a Junior Rider soon," she said as she left in a huff, taking her new badge to show her mom.

Chapter 3
The Caper Begins

Throughout September, Jeremy and Jordan settled into their usual routine of school, chores, Frolic Riders meetings and homework. As the leaves started changing colors, they realized winter wasn't too far away, which meant they wouldn't be able to ride their horses as often as they wanted.

Even so, fall was one of Jordan and Jeremy's favorite times of the year, in spite of being back in school. Most days, as soon as the school bus dropped them off, the boys changed clothes, then sat at the kitchen table and ate a snack, usually fruit, rarely cookies, which they preferred. Then, they headed outside to ride and play before it got too dark outside, unless they had homework to finish.

On many cool Saturday nights throughout the fall, the family enjoyed building a campfire in their fire pit, drinking hot cider or hot cocoa, and roasting marshmallows. Sometimes they cooked hot dogs on a stick over the glowing embers. Jordan and Jeremy loved eating dinner at the campfire pit. They often invited Chip, Molly, and their parents to join them. If it was nice weather, Chip was sometimes allowed to spend the night, and the three boys slept in sleeping bags in the tree house. Of course, every time the boys got to do this, Molly begged to join them but the answer was always "No!"

On Sunday mornings, Jeremy and Jordan usually woke up to the delicious aroma of bacon and eggs, or sometimes pancakes and sausages, then went to church. In the afternoons, they were allowed to play outside and spend time with their horses. They never seemed to get tired of trail riding. Jeremy liked to practice with the lariat, and they played cowboys and Indians, or cavalry versus Indians.

Sometimes they practiced their riding techniques in the ring, with their mom giving them pointers. She had given up on either of her sons being interested in showing, except for the Riders shows, but realized it was more important that the boys just had fun with the horses, and she had to admit, they were both becoming very skilled riders.

Sunday evenings were for family time, and unless the boys had a lot of homework to finish, they played board games, popped popcorn, and sometimes watched a movie together. Banner and Penny also enjoyed Sundays, and grazed happily in the pasture. Much as they loved their human friends, it was nice for them that they got to relax, too.

Jeremy practiced the piano daily, and had a lesson every week, which was why he was so good and also why Jordan was constantly confused as to how Jeremy could stand practicing piano instead of playing video games. But, he had to admit (to himself, that is) that Jeremy was pretty good; though he never told Jeremy. Sometimes, Jordan actually enjoyed listening to him, except when he played the same thing over and over again.

"Play something else!" he would yell whenever Jeremy started practicing scales.

"In a minute!" Jeremy would yell back and then break into arpeggios to really annoy Jordan.

One day, in early October Jordan happened to be looking at the newspaper; he wasn't actually reading it, but was looking for an article for his social studies assignment. An article about a car theft ring in the neighboring town of New Austin caught his eye. The story said that cars were being stolen out of people's driveways and parking lots, in broad daylight. The stolen cars were taken somewhere – called a "Chop Shop" – where they were repainted and then used as get-away cars in robberies. A 2001 GMC Jimmy, which was stolen from someone's garage in July, was identified as the vehicle used in a bank robbery last August in Flint, 50 miles away from Frolicville.

Jordan tore the article out of the newspaper and stuffed it in his notebook. Then, he and Jeremy rushed out of the house to catch the bus.

"Hey, have you heard about the cars that are being stolen around here?" Jordan asked Chip once they all got settled in the bus for the long ride to school.

"I heard that Mr. Grimmer got his old SUV stolen right from his garage last summer." Chip said. "I overheard my dad talking on the phone to him right after it happened."

"Maybe that's why he's been so grumpy at our meetings," Jeremy said from the seat behind them as he rested his chin on the top of their seat.

"Could be, "Chip said. "But, that's not the best part of this story. I know who's doing it. I tried to tell my dad so we could tell the police, but he told me it was just my imagination. Then, he gave me a lecture about the dangers of accusing people of things they didn't do, and I just forgot about it."

"Can I see the article, Jordan?" Molly asked from the seat across the aisle.

"Yeah, I 'spose," Jordan said as he took it out of his pocket. While Molly read the article, Jordan turned to Chip and said. "What d'ya mean, you know who's doing it?"

"It's old man Carson! I know it's him!"

"What are you talking about, Chip? You crazy? What makes you think your neighbor is running a chop shop? And why haven't you ever said anything to us about it? Jordan whispered loudly.

"Think about Carson's property. Why else would he have a high privacy fence like that, and keep the gate closed and locked all the time so you can't see in? But I can see what he's doing right from our front porch. Plus, me and Rocket get pretty close to his property every time I ride. After I found out about Mr. Grimmer's car being stolen, I started noticing how sneaky Mr. Carson looked whenever he opened or closed that gate. So I started watching the place and riding past it really slow. I must've seen 30 different cars goin' in and out of that gate last summer. It sure looks shady to me!" Chip exclaimed.

"I've seen you spying on him, now I know why!" Molly commented as she looked up from the newspaper article. "You think he's the car thief in this story!"

"First of all," Jordan said, "I can't believe you were spying on him all summer and didn't tell us. Besides, he could have dogs or something else he doesn't want to let escape, or maybe he just wants privacy for some reason."

"Second of all, you couldn't have seen all those cars coming and going when you were riding Rocket. Mr. Carson would have seen you. So, how else do you know about so many cars coming in, Chip?" Jordan continued. "Don't tell me you've been sittin' there in your living room watchin' out the window all the time!" Jordan said.

Chip replied, "No way. I just wait until Jake barks. That gate has a rusty hinge that squeaks real loud every time they open it, and Jake hates it. He doesn't like old man Carson either. I just know something's going on over there."

Chip crossed his arms and turned his head in a huff to look out the window, but then realized he had more to say.

"That's the kind of stuff I thought you'd say so I didn't tell you guys. But, since you brought it up, just think about it – even if he does have dogs or needs privacy, it still doesn't explain all those cars going in. I saw a ratty old flatbed truck haul a couple of junk cars out of there just last week, now that you mention it. Old man Carson probably stripped them. Let me have that article, Molly. I'm gonna show it to dad when he comes home this weekend. Then, I'm gonna tell him about all the stuff I've seen going on at Carson's since Mr. Grimmer got his car stolen."

That was all it took for all three of them – Molly, Jeremy and Jordan – to be convinced that there was something fishy going on at the Carson place. "OK, Jordan said, "Let's wait 'til after school on Friday to tell our parents. They'll know what to do."

That Saturday morning, Jordan and Jeremy met up on horseback with Chip; Molly tagged along as usual. One look at the brothers' faces told Chip that they had run into the same problem he and Molly had.

Molly spoke first. "Our parents told us to mind our own business, that Mr. Carson probably built the fence to keep out Chip's footballs and baseballs that always seem to end up in his yard."

Jordan agreed, "Yeah, our folks told us he probably just wants his privacy, and it's probably just some old junk cars he had in his backyard. But I think there's something going on there. Guess we'll have to prove it on our own."

"Yeah!" Chip said, "I think it's our duty as Junior Riders to expose old man Carson and his criminal friends. But how?"

"We'll have to find proof somehow," Jeremy stated. "Then they'll have to believe us."

"We'll find that proof. Let's think on it while we ride," Chip said as the others nodded their heads in agreement. They liked the idea of being private investigators.

The four of them rode together, along the bank of Skeleton Creek, and followed it as it meandered all the way to Mr. Carson's property. Even on horseback, they couldn't see over his fence. At a shallow part of the creek, they had the horses wade across. Rocket balked and fussed over crossing the creek, and it took all of Chip's patience to get him across while the others waited for them. They rode their horses slowly down the field next to Mr. Carson's fence line, and looked for gaps in the fence. All they found were a couple of knotholes that were too high for them to see through. The fall rains made the ground soggy in places.

They continued on around the back of the property, where they wouldn't be seen by anyone driving by on the road. They finally found a good-sized knothole, but it was quite high up on the fence. Even sitting on Rocket, the tallest horse, Chip could not see through the hole.

"Someone could stand up on their horse and see through it, I bet. I would try, but Rocket is a little jumpy, you know."

Jeremy pointed out helpfully, "Jordan could stand on top of Banner's saddle and peer through the hole. Banner is very steady."

"Thanks a lot," his brother muttered, but he took a deep breath, maneuvered Banner next to the hole, firmly told him "Whoa!" and stood up in the saddle. He steadied himself against the fence with one hand, but there was nothing to grab onto as he cautiously peered through the hole.

"There's a Ford Taurus," he whispered, "and some other beat up clunkers that are stripped to their frames. Wait a minute.....wait a minute, Oh Wow!" He whispered!

Suddenly, he saw Mr. Carson come out of the storage barn and walk toward one of the cars. It startled Jordan, so he jerked a little. This caused his foot to slip off the saddle, which alarmed Banner. Banner sidled away, and Jordan fell splat on his backside onto the mucky ground. Luckily, the mud muffled the noise. Motioning to his friends to be quiet, he remounted Banner, and they all rode away from Carson's place so he wouldn't hear them.

When it was safe, Jeremy whispered, "Mom's gonna kill you for getting so dirty." Jordan's shirt, boots, and the seat of his pants were very muddy, but he was unhurt.

"Won't be the first time," Jordan said.

"Never mind that. Wait'll you hear what all I saw!" Jordan paused for effect. "Now we know for sure that something's going on there. Carson has a red sports car that looks like a Corvette and I think a red Porsche too! I've never seen Mr. Carson driving a bright red sports car like that, have you guys? Plus, there were one or two other sporty cars too. I've only seen him drive that big old blue pickup. Those sports cars must be stolen. And those other cars have been stripped."

Molly piped up, "Maybe he's just fixing people's cars for them."

"If he was running a legit car repair shop, he'd have a sign out front and wouldn't keep it a secret," Jeremy commented.

"So what do we do? Call the police ourselves and report that there's a stolen car ring operating out of our neighbor's house?" Molly asked.

"The cops won't take us seriously. And we can't tell our folks what Jordan saw today, because they already told us to stay out of Mr. Carson's business and we'll be busted for sure." Chip explained.

"I know what to do," Jordan piped up. We'll write a letter to the Frolicville Chief of Police and sign it anonymous, and mail it to the police station! They'll come and arrest Mr. Carson, just like on TV!"

The others agreed it was worth a try anyway, and decided Jordan and Jeremy were the best writers. "When we're working on the case, we can call it the Skeleton Creek Caper!" Jeremy added. The others all liked that idea.

It was getting late, so they split up and headed for home.

When Jordan and Jeremy came to the bridge over Skeleton Creek, Jordan decided to wash off some of the mud on his clothes. He dismounted and was bending over, when Banner nudged him, none too gently. Jordan fell over, face first, into Skeleton Creek. Jeremy laughed, but Jordan scolded Banner as he picked himself out of the water. All of a sudden, he noticed a shiny grayish object near his left foot, and he reached in to pull it out. Jeremy shouted out, "Stop, it's a bone! Don't touch it! Eeww! Now we know why it's called Skeleton Creek!"

"It's not a bone. It's just a license plate with a few weeds on it, for Pete's sake." Jordan held up a crumpled up license plate covered with weeds and mud. "I bet this is from a stolen car at Carson's place!"

Jeremy said excitedly, "Yeah. We'll have to get the police to run the license plate number. Just like on TV!"

The boys rode home, and managed to sneak into the house with the license plate hidden under Jordan's damp shirt. He changed clothes quickly. Jordan and Jeremy sat at the computer to write the letter, which made their mom happy to see them working away together. It was nice to see them getting along. She thought they were doing homework, knowing that Jordan had a writing project that was due Monday.

Jordan printed out the letter, then read it to Jeremy.

Dear Police Chief:

Mr. Carson, of Frolicville, is running the chop shop. I have seen stolen cars on his property and found a license plate in Skeleton Creek, which is probably from one of the cars he stole. The license plate number is ABX3490.

Anonymous

When he was done reading the letter, he folded it and put it in an envelope that Jeremy had addressed. "We'll mail it Monday – we'll slip it in the mailbox on our way to the bus," Jordan said.

"It's perfect," Jeremy said.

On Monday morning, both boys were up bright and early. As usual, Jordan was rushing to try to get his writing assignment finished. He paid Jeremy $2.00 to do his chores – feed and water the horses, Laddie and the barn cats – so he could have more time. True to Jordan's dad's words, Jordan would be a world-class procrastinator, if he ever got around to it.

Jeremy did Jordan's chores and his own, which today was to clean both stalls. By the time he was back in the house, Jordan had finished his writing assignment, more or less (it could have used a good proofreading), and grabbed a postage stamp for their letter. The boys sat down for a hearty breakfast of cinnamon-flavored oatmeal with raisins, toast with peanut butter, orange juice, and a tall glass of cold milk. They made their own sack lunches, since they only ordered the hot lunch on Fridays, which was pizza day.

Jordan and Jeremy ran down the driveway as soon as they saw the bus coming down their road. Jordan slipped their letter in the mailbox; luckily the little flag was up already, because their dad was mailing out bill payments. They clambered up the steps into the bus. Jordan sat down next to Chip, and Jeremy sat in the seat behind them. Chip listened as Jordan reported finding the license plate, and was thrilled that the letter was written and mailed already.

Jordan said confidently, "Now we just wait for the police to take care of it. They'll get to the bottom of it."

Chip told them he would be watching for the police to arrive in about two days, and would call them as soon as he saw them.

Jeremy asked hopefully, "Do you think they'll put the sirens on, and the lights? Maybe we'll be able to hear it from our house."

"I dunno," Chip replied. "Maybe."

Molly piped up from the seat in front of Jordan and Chip, "We might not even be home. We might be at school!"

Soon the bus pulled up in front of the school, and the kids had other things to think about. Jordan was feeling a little guilty about the slapdash job he did on the writing assignment, until he mentioned it to Chip, who had somehow forgotten all about it. Jordan felt lots better then.

For the next two days, Jordan and Jeremy were quick to saddle up and ride over to Chip and Molly's farm, to keep an eye out for the police.

On Wednesday, they arrived to find Chip half-heartedly raking leaves and Jake watching him. They helped him out by jumping in the piles of leaves that he had raked.

The children were getting tired of waiting for the police to arrive; Molly couldn't stand it anymore. On Thursday, after school, she broke down and asked her mom if the police had been over to Mr. Carson's house. Suspicious, her mom replied "No, and why would you think such a thing, Molly?"

"Oh, I don't know. Nothing exciting happens around here," Molly hedged a bit.

"Well," her mom replied, "It would be exciting for me if you would clean up your room and put away all your toys. While Chip is raking, you can get started."

Glumly, Molly went to her room and started putting away her toys. She knew better than to argue with her mom when she had that tone in her voice. She had just finished putting away her clean clothes that were lying in a heap on the floor, when she heard Chip talking to Jordan and Jeremy. With her room almost clean, Molly raced downstairs to see what was going on.

"Absolutely nothing," Chip was saying. "No cops at all. And I saw some cars go in there late last night again. Jake always barks when the gate opens over there, because it squeaks pretty loud you know, and he woke me up. I peeked out the window and saw two more cars drive in."

Jordan sighed and said, "I guess we'll just have to wait and see what happens. I hope Mr. Carson doesn't oil that squeaky hinge."

Chip added, "I give Jake a treat every time he barks when that gate squeaks. He's getting pretty well trained."

It was hard, but the children managed to spend the next week without going over to Carson's to investigate. Jordan had to rewrite his assignment after he got a D on it, and that wasted a whole evening by the time both parents proofread and critiqued it. His parents were not happy with a D, and told him he would be grounded for a week if he got another one. Jeremy practiced the piano diligently and was becoming "an excellent pianist", according to his piano teacher.

Both boys did find time to ride their horses in their own corral, with their mom giving them a few pointers. They were getting ready for the Frolic Riders fall gymkhana. This was a type of horse show that consisted of games for all levels of horses and riders. It also included a special exhibition by the drill team – a routine to music – and a vaulting team demonstration.

The boys thought gymnastics on horseback was really cool; they couldn't believe what they were seeing every time they watched a rider actually stand on the horse's back, then do flips and handstands and other exciting tricks. Of course, they thought it was way cooler when a rider fell off the horse, which was probably what made it interesting to watch.

On the day of the gymkhana, all of the children were dressed in their official Rider or Cadet uniforms and mounted on their shiny clean horses. They rode proudly around the arena in pairs, to a marching tune. The group was led by several of the Elite Riders, who made up the color guard. Chip noticed that one of the parents in the audience was the Chief of Police in Frolicville.

"Look, there's Chief Morgan, from Frolicville. Keep your eye on him," Chip whispered to Jordan, who was riding Banner next to him.

Rocket noticed Chip wasn't paying attention and took advantage of it to stop and crane his neck around so he could scratch an itchy spot on his hind leg. The troop behind them had to stop and wait for Chip and Rocket to get going again. Chip looked up and saw that he and Rocket were holding up the procession and heard giggles from the audience as he and Rocket hurried to catch up with Banner and Jordan.

Overall, the kids enjoyed the opening ceremony. Most of the horses behaved well, but a few of the newer horses spooked at some of the flags waving, as they left the arena.

The games were fun for the riders and audience and most of the horses and ponies seemed to enjoy themselves as well. The boot race for the Cadets was hilarious. One boot from each Cadet was placed at one end of the arena, and the Cadets raced on their ponies to find their own boot, put it back on, and make it to the finish line first. Molly won this event; she was quick to find her boot, jam it on her foot, jump on Midnight, and race back to cross the finish line. Some of the younger Cadets were still trying to get back on their prancing ponies long after Molly had finished.

Next up for the boot race were the Junior Riders. Jeremy and Penny did very well, and came in 2nd place. Jordan and Banner weren't allowed to participate in these types of running events, because Jordan's mom was afraid Banner might get injured. Since Banner was a highly-trained former dressage show horse, he had to be treated more carefully. Jordan understood, and watched and cheered on his friends.

Chip and Rocket were the first team to arrive at the pile of boots, but Chip's boot was a little tight and he had trouble getting into it. Chip hopped up and down, trying to jam his foot into his boot. He accidentally let go of Rocket's reins, who then promptly took off. One of the Elite Riders tracked Rocket down and brought him back to Chip. The race was over by the time Chip remounted and raced back.

The next event for the Junior Riders was the egg race. This wasn't really a race at all; the children rode around the arena holding a raw egg in a spoon in one hand, and the reins in the other hand. The object was to be the last Junior Rider still balancing the egg, without touching it with fingers. Some of the less-well-trained horses had a hard time in this event.

Banner and Jordan were allowed to compete in this event because speed was not involved, and Banner usually did very well. Mr. Grimmer came around to each rider and put a raw egg into his or her spoon. When he came to Chip and Rocket, almost as soon as he put the egg in the spoon, Chip let out a big sloppy sneeze, and dropped the egg splat onto Mr. Grimmer's freshly-polished boots. Chip apologized, and was given a new egg. "Hang onto it this time, Chip," ordered Mr. Grimmer.

Then the command to walk was given. Most of the Junior Riders managed to hold onto their eggs during this part. But, once they were told to trot, the eggs started dropping quickly. Chip dropped his very quickly, and got gooey egg all over his pants. Jeremy dropped his egg too, but it landed on the ground. By the time they started to canter, Jordan and Banner were the only ones left. Jordan was proud to accept a blue ribbon for the victory.

Penny and Jeremy were also doing well. Penny was good at the speed and action events. She was quick like a cat, and handled well. Jeremy's main job was to hang on while she sped through the events. Penny was especially good at the barrel race; she looked like a red streak as she rounded the barrels and won the barrel race for their age group. With two wins, the Chambers boys were very pleased with their results.

After their events were finished, they cooled out their horses and put them back in their trailers, then lined up along the fence to watch the vaulting team exhibition. They also noticed the Frolicville Chief of Police standing near a tall, long-haired, very pretty Elite Rider.

Jordan pointed out, "She's the Police Chief's daughter, Amanda Morgan, and she's the vaulting team captain. I think she shows her horse most of the summer too." Chip just stared, open-mouthed, at the pretty young lady. Jeremy stared at her beautiful palomino horse.

Then, out of nowhere, Molly exclaimed, "That's it! One of us has to join the vaulting team so we can get to know Amanda. Then we can tell her about Mr. Carson so she can convince her dad to look into it!"

"Great idea, Molly! Do you want to join the vaulting team?" Chip asked sarcastically, knowing that Molly could barely turn a somersault, much less acrobatics on horseback.

Jeremy said, "Molly's right. It's a great idea. Who is the best gymnast among us?" he asked as he quickly turned to look at Jordan. Jordan was always showing off, doing cartwheels, flips, climbing and swinging on their rope to the tree house.

Molly and Chip quickly turned to look at Jordan too.

"Oh no! Not me!! That's suicidal!" Jordan exclaimed.

Molly said, "Oh, come on, Jordan. It's not that dangerous, and we really need you. It's either you or Chip and we all know Chip is too klutzy."

Jeremy piped up, "Yeah, don't be chicken, Jordan." Jordan quickly popped his brother hard on the arm with his knuckles, careful to make sure their parents weren't watching.

Even Chip turned traitor and said, "Let's find out when your first practice is!"

Then, they all raced over to the vaulters, who were exiting the riding arena. Jordan noticed that one vaulter was limping, and looked like he'd taken a bath in the sawdust covering the arena floor.

"Oh, boy, I'm doomed," Jordan muttered to himself, then added, "Maybe Mom won't let me take Banner. It might be too hard on him," Jordan said hopefully.

Jeremy found their mom quickly and asked her if Banner and Jordan could join the vaulting team. To Jordan's chagrin, she gave him permission, and he forced a sickly smile on his face. His first practice was in a week. Jordan had a sinking feeling in the pit of his stomach, but was determined to make the best of it.

Chapter 4

Halloween Treats

Halloween season was definitely one of the kids' favorite times of year. The weather was cool, but not too cold to be outside, as long as it didn't rain. Two days before Halloween, on one of the rare nights when Molly and Chip's parents went out for what they called "a date", Molly and Chip had been invited to stay for dinner with Jordan and Jeremy. As they waited for dinner to be ready, Chip and Jordan hung out in the tree house, making final plans for their Halloween costumes. Jeremy was practicing the piano in the house and, as usual, Molly stood below, complaining because they didn't let her join them.

"No girls allowed," Chip called down to his sister. Deep in important conversation about their costumes, the boys didn't notice what Molly was up to. The little girl was small, but resourceful. Disappearing into the tack room, she emerged with a stepstool and molasses. She had seen the boys pour molasses over grain as a special treat for Banner and Penny, and knew where to find it.

Now, it's important to know that molasses is very sticky. Standing on the stepstool, Molly quickly rolled up the rope ladder, tied it in triple knots, and then painted sticky molasses on the knots with a paint stirrer.

Then she took the end of the climbing rope and carried it to a nearby maple tree. She tied it to a sturdy branch while standing on a stepstool, then sat down on the stepstool to wait.

She didn't wait very long. She heard the piano playing stop, and then Jordan's mom called them to dinner.

Molly innocently skipped inside and washed her hands. She peeked out the window to see the fun. Sure enough, the boys tried to shake the climbing rope down, but Molly had tied it too securely. The knot-tying practice at some of the Frolic Riders meetings had really paid off. Chip tried to climb down the rope ladder. When he hit the knots, he struggled to untie them. The molasses made it hard, but he finally managed to untie and release the ladder, and climbed down.

Chip had been wearing a pale yellow sweatshirt over an old ratty t-shirt, which his mom wanted him to throw out. He took off his sweatshirt and wiped the molasses off his face and hands as best as he could. Jordan, meanwhile, climbed down behind him. Although his hands were gooey, his clothes hadn't suffered much. "You look like you just went swimming in a mud pond," Jordan said, laughing.

Chip's face flushed in anger and frustration. "That darn Molly," he fumed.

"Maybe we should have let her come up," Jordan said.

"Never! Especially now!" Chip declared.

The boys washed up at the bathroom sink and joined Jeremy and Molly at the dinner table. Mrs. Chambers took one look at Chip, and knowing Chip, didn't even bother to ask what happened to him. Instead, she said, "Jordan, you're about the same size as Chip. You have several nice shirts you never wear. Why don't you go and get one for Chip? He looks uncomfortable."

"OK," Jordan agreed. He and Chip had decided not to rat on Molly. She might tell about all the chips and candy they had stashed in the tree house. Or, worse yet, she might tell her parents about spying on Mr. Carson and sending the letter to the police with the evidence they collected.

"There's only one way to keep Molly from botherin' us anymore," Chip said. "And that's to give her an assignment so she feels like she's part of the Skeleton Creek caper. "

"Good thinking," Jordan said, "But what can an eight year old do?"

"Well, she's smart and nosy."

"Yeah, so is Jeremy," Jordan said. "Hey! I've got it! Let's tell Molly and Jeremy that they're the investigative reporters. Their job is to collect evidence . . . they have to check the Frolicville newspaper and try to watch the news to catch stories about cars being stolen, or stolen cars being used in robberies and stuff."

"Perfect!" Chip said. "That'll keep her out of our hair and actually, she and Jeremy would be doin' somethin' that could help us get Carson busted."

"OK. Tonight, you tell Molly and I'll tell Jeremy. Now, let's go eat! I'm starving!"

After a tasty dinner of cheeseburgers hot off the grill, chips, baked beans, and potato salad, Molly and Chip went upstairs to Jordan's bedroom to goof around while they waited for their parents to pick them up.

Kicking some dirty clothes under his bed, Jordan went toward his desk where his allowance money was lying out. He took the nine one dollar bills and split them between three canisters that were covered with pictures he had cut out and pasted onto them.

Intrigued by the canisters, Molly asked him, "These are pretty cool. What are they for, Jordan?"

"They're for my allowance. We split the money into each canister, a third each. This first one has a picture of a church on it. That's the "Give" jar. I give that to our church."

Jeremy piped up, "Sometimes we give to the Red Cross. I have canisters for my allowance too."

Jordan continued, "Another third of my allowance goes into this "Grow" canister. See, I've got a picture of an Ipod on it. I'm saving up to buy an Ipod, which is gonna take a while."

Chip asked, "What about this other canister? It says "Get" and has dollar signs on it."

Jordan replied, "Oh, that's my spending money. I'll get something at the store with that."

"I get it," Molly said. "Give, Grow, Get. That's really cool. Chip gets an allowance sometimes, but he just spends it all. I'm going to tell my mom about Give, Grow, Get. Maybe I'll get an allowance too."

"Shut up, Molly!" Chip said, "I have a piggy bank, and I put money in there . . . sometimes."

Just then, Mrs. Chambers yelled for Chip and Molly to come down. Their parents had arrived. All four kids ran down the stairs, sounding almost as loud at their horses.

As Jordan and Chip said good-bye, they winked at each other as a way of saying "Yep, we're on it – we've got two investigative reporters on our team!"

Halloween finally arrived. Molly was Annie Oakley, Chip was Sir Lancelot, with a cardboard sword and shield, Jordan was the Lone Ranger, and Jeremy was Tonto, dressed in Indian garb complete with a feather in his headband.

The four of them went trick or treating on horseback, while Mrs. Chambers and Mrs. Easton followed behind in the Chambers' SUV. As each kid was given candy, each horse received an apple or a carrot. As they rode from one house to the next, which was a very long distance, they had plenty of time and privacy to discuss what Molly and Jeremy had found out in the past two days that would help them in their Skeleton Creek Caper.

Chapter 5

Winter Fun and Christmas Time

The rest of fall was busy for Chip and Molly, but Jordan and Jeremy were especially busy; in addition to the Riders meetings, Jeremy had piano practice and Jordan had vaulting team practice. And, since he was new to the team, he had to work three times harder (and fall ten times more) just to get caught up with the others.

So, while Jordan was doing his part in the caper, and Molly and Jeremy were busy gathering information, Chip continued to watch the activity going on at Mr. Carson's. Every day, as they rode the bus to school, Chip reported what he had seen. Sometimes, a whole week would go by with nothing happening. But, on those mornings when Chip had something to report, he went into great detail.

"At about 10:00 last night, Jake barked and woke me up. I tiptoed through the house and went out onto the porch. Sure enough, the squeaky gate opened and I saw the round headlights of a car driving into his driveway. It was really dark and cold so I couldn't see much and I couldn't stay out there for very long. But, I saw enough. Now, what do you have to report? How long do we have to wait before we can go to Police Chief Morgan?"

"Well," said Jordan. "I've been able to talk to his daughter Amanda a few times at vaulting team practice."

"You actually talk to Amanda!" Chip said as his eyes got bigger.

"Relax! I just make up questions to ask her about how to do a certain trick or when our next practice is. But, I don't know her well enough to ask her to talk to her father about paying a visit to Mr. Carson. She barely knows my name!"

"Well, hurry up. The longer we wait, the more cars that are stolen," Molly said. "Since Halloween, there have been four more thefts in the county."

"And, don't forget about that gas station robbery that happened in New Austin. It said in the paper that the car the robbers drove was probably stolen," Jeremy added.

"OK, OK!" Jordan said rolling his eyes. "I'm doing the best I can!"

This is how it went throughout November. And then, before they knew it, it was Thanksgiving, which to them meant a delicious meal with their grandparents, aunts, uncles and cousins and a mini-vacation from school. However, Mrs. Chambers made sure the boys didn't spend all their vacation time playing; on the day after Thanksgiving, she took them to the library to check out some new books and DVDs. Jeremy chose a Sherlock Holmes book and Jordan checked out a book about sports cars that had pictures of some of the models Chip said he had seen on Mr. Carson's property.

But, in addition to a turkey dinner and time off from school, Thanksgiving also meant that winter and Christmas were coming! And, since they couldn't ride their horses much, Jordan and Jeremy had plenty of time for sledding down the big hill at the township park and ice skating on their frozen pond, often with Chip and Molly. Sometimes to warm up afterwards, Mrs. Chambers would invite them all in for steaming hot mugs of cocoa, and chocolate chip cookies just out of the oven.

One clear, but cold December Saturday, both families skated together on the pond. It was one of the rare weekends when Chip and Molly's dad was home. Mr. Chambers built a roaring bonfire, and they drank hot cider and ate cookies, donuts, and toasted marshmallows until way past the kids' bedtimes. Reluctantly, Chip and Molly left with their parents. They loved it when they all got to do things together and after a night like that one, Chip and Molly wished even more that their dad could be home every night.

About a week later, Jeremy had a Christmas piano recital, and played without making any mistakes. Jordan suffered through it. He hated getting dressed up. His suit was a little tight, and ties always felt like they were choking him. But, he had to admit that Jeremy did a good job and he noticed that Jeremy seemed to stand just a little taller as he took his bows in front of the audience.

The best part after a recital – for both boys – was going out for dinner, a treat they didn't get very often. As they were riding home in the car, Jordan started talking about his vaulting lessons.

His mom said they were looking forward to watching his spring exhibition and his dad added that that there would be another restaurant celebration after that event.

"It's awesome the way some of the kids can stand on top of the horse and flip – even when they're cantering in a circle! I'm getting used to it; I can almost stand on my horse's back at a walk. But, I can only land on my feet on the flying dismount some of the time," Jordan said as he remembered how sore and bruised he got after every practice, which made him thankful for the icepacks his mom kept in the freezer.

As he thought more and more about how hard – and painful – vaulting practice was, he reminded himself that he had to stick it out because Riders are tough and don't quit, and he had a crime to solve.

Later, about a week before Christmas vacation, while doing barn chores, Jeremy asked him, "So, how's it going with talking to Amanda about the Skeleton Creek caper?"

"I haven't been able to talk to her yet." Jordan replied. "But she's going to teach the beginners the next trick, which is the running mount. I'm planning to talk to her then."

Jordan didn't let on to Jeremy that he was a bit scared of the running mount, which is when the vaulting horse canters slowly around the circle as the rider runs alongside, and with perfect timing, gracefully swings onto the horse using the handholds on the surcingle. And even though Jordan and the other beginners would start at the walk, it was still a bit scary.

The boys finished their chores in the barn, and then raced each other to the house, where they knew their mom was making spaghetti and meatballs for dinner.

The next day in school, Jordan talked to Chip about a strategy for getting to talk to Amanda. Unfortunately, their teacher noticed them too, and gave them a stern warning. "It doesn't look to me like you're working on your math assignment," their teacher scolded.

With his eyes back down on his paper, Jordan whispered to Chip that he would help him finish the assignment on the bus. He knew Chip had enough trouble with math already.

That night, Jordan and Jeremy both worked hard on their Riders assignments for their next badge. They had to learn the parts of the horse for the test at Saturday's meeting. Before going to bed, their mom quizzed them; they knew the answers.

The Riders meeting went well. Jordan and Jeremy both achieved their badge after correctly pointing out and naming the parts of the horse. Chip did not fare so well, and would need to study more before the next meeting. Molly offered to help him, which only made matters worse.

Meanwhile, the vaulting team met right after the full Rider meeting, to lay plans for the spring Frolic Riders horse show and special exhibition. Jordan made sure to sit as close to Amanda as he could, looking for an opportunity to talk to her alone.

The leaders told the beginner vaulters that they could help the more experienced vaulters, but that they wouldn't actually be in the exhibition yet. Jordan was relieved because he knew he'd need a lot more practice before he could perform in public. He had no chance to talk to Amanda, but some of his efforts were rewarded with a quick smile she shot his way before she left. He noticed that Amanda was driving a car, and realized she had to be at least sixteen. No wonder it was hard to talk to her – why would a sixteen year old girl talk to an eleven year old boy?

Christmas vacation arrived at last. Without really saying it, Jordan, Jeremy, Chip and Molly knew they would have to put their crime solving activities on hold for a while. It was time for fun!

The Chambers had many family traditions to uphold during the holiday season. Mr. and Mrs. Chambers were off work for a week before Christmas and the boys' grandparents visited, which both boys really enjoyed. Jordan and Jeremy especially liked going to the thick wooded part of their property, to pick out their Christmas tree. The boys rode double on Banner, while their dad and grandfather walked alongside. There was just enough snow to bring their sled. Soon they found several nice small trees, close enough to Skeleton Creek to hear that it wasn't frozen yet. They had a hard time agreeing on a tree; they each selected a different tree as the very best.

Finally, they agreed on the one their grandpa picked, and their dad quickly chopped it down with his ax. They tied it onto the sled and Banner towed it back. Once they got it into their garage, their dad shook off the snow and trimmed a couple of the branches. Their dad and grandpa carried it into the house and set it up in the stand in front of the picture window. Their mom and grandma had brought out the Christmas decorations, and offered steaming mugs of cider. They all decorated the tree, and sang while Jeremy played their favorite Christmas songs on the piano. Later that night, they played Monopoly in front of a roaring fire in the fireplace.

The next day dawned clear and cold, but not as shivery cold as the previous day. Jordan and Jeremy had fun with their grandparents, especially when they told them about some of the pranks their dad had pulled when he was their age. Jordan listened very carefully, and got some ideas for some future stunts. Reading his older son's mind, Mr. Chambers was quick to tell both boys that they weren't to try any of the things he had done.

"We know, Dad," Jordan responded, while planning out the first prank he'd pull on Jeremy.

Then their mom announced that she had a special treat planned; they were going for a sleigh ride with Banner as their driving horse!

"Now we'll really see what kind of shape you've got Banner in, Jordan. Pulling all four of us in the sleigh will be harder for him than when you boys were little," Mrs. Chambers joked.

Their grandparents opted to stay inside the warm house. "Besides," their grandma said, "someone has to take the photos."

Mrs. Chambers asked the boys to bring the horses into the barn, and then groom Banner, which they did in record time. Their mom carefully harnessed Banner, while their dad pulled the sleigh onto their driveway. The sleigh was shiny black, with a red velvet seat cushion, and a warm, plaid blanket as a lap robe.

Mrs. Chambers maneuvered Banner into position, and hitched him to the sleigh. Then she added his sleigh bells. For safety's sake, she drove him a few steps before she let anyone climb into the sleigh. When she was sure all was well with Banner, she climbed in and held the reins snugly to keep Banner still. Jordan, Jeremy, and their dad squeezed in. Jordan thought the seat seemed a little smaller than last year and figured out it must be because he had gotten so much bigger.

They all snuggled together as they pulled the blanket up around them, and then their grandmother came out to take pictures. They posed for several photos before Banner started getting impatient. They started down the road at a walk at first, to limber him up, and soon began a brisk trot. Waving goodbye to their grandparents, Jordan could see his grandma still snapping photos.

It was a beautiful sunny day, with a bright blue sky, and shining white snow. Banner kept up a steady trot as the Chambers traveled down the road, waving to neighbors. Soon the family was singing Christmas carols, with the sleigh bells as accompaniment. Jordan and Jeremy knew they would always remember this day. They only got the sleigh out a couple of times each year, and it was always such a treat. Banner seemed to be enjoying himself too; he held his head and tail high as he pranced down the road at a trot.

Before they knew it, it was time to head for home. Mrs. Chambers slowed Banner to a walk when they neared their farm, because she wanted to cool him down properly so he wouldn't get chilled. Even so, when they got back to the barn and Banner was unhitched then unharnessed, Jordan and Jeremy rubbed him down. They blanketed him when they put him back in his stall. The boys were allowed to give Banner some hay, but no water or grain until he was cooled down completely. Their mom fed Banner a couple of carrots as a reward for his good behavior. Penny had been acting jealous, so Jeremy made it up to her with a little extra food.

The boys followed their parents to the house. Carrying hot mugs of cocoa, they settled into chairs around the dining room table and were soon engrossed in a game of Monopoly with their grandparents. Jordan won, and then they all enjoyed a pizza for dinner.

Mrs. Chambers and the boys soon went out to check on Banner and Penny, then watered and fed them grain and a generous portion of hay. Back in the house again, Jeremy started practicing the piano, playing mostly Christmas pieces, while Jordan took the opportunity to call Chip. He wanted to know if anything had gone on at Mr. Carson's place.

When Jordan told Chip about the fun they had on the sleigh ride, Chip was a little envious. They didn't own a sleigh, and Rocket didn't know how to pull one anyway.

"I didn't see any cars going in or out of the gate, let alone cars that looked like they'd been stolen, when we drove past Carson's place in the sleigh."

"I haven't seen anything going on over there either, so maybe old man Carson went away for the holidays," Chip added.

Just then, Jordan's grandpa came into the room, so Jordan cut the call short. "Hey, Grandpa, are you ready to play cards?" He knew his grandpa loved playing cards, so he figured it would distract him from the telephone conversation, but he had no such luck this time.

"Jordan, what were you talking about with Chip? Something about stolen cars?" His grandfather asked.

"Oh, just some of the neighbors down the road. They have a lot of cars going in and out," Jordan explained.

Just his luck, his dad walked in on that conversation, and got angry.

"Jordan, don't start on that again. There is nothing wrong with Mr. Carson having visitors drive in from time to time. He certainly isn't running a criminal enterprise out of his back yard. For Pete's sake, this is a normal neighborhood; our neighbors aren't crooks!"

Jordan spoke up, "But, Dad, we just know something's going on there, and we want to get to the bottom of it."

"That's enough, Jordan. You kids need to mind your own business, and leave Mr. Carson alone. He complains enough about Chip and Molly riding and playing too close to his property."

A little embarrassed, Jordan said, "OK, Dad."

"Geez," Jordan thought to himself as his dad walked away, "It sure is hard to be a private investigator, when no one takes you seriously."

Then, he went to the den and played cards with Jeremy and his grandparents until it was time for dinner.

And, then, it was Christmas! Even though they were getting older, they loved getting the presents Santa Claus still seemed to bring them. On Christmas Eve, they went to church where Jeremy played a beautiful

Christmas selection, once again without making any mistakes, in front of the whole congregation. He even sang a solo with the children's choir. Jordan was a little annoyed with all the attention his brother received after the service.

On Christmas day, both boys sprang out of bed and raced downstairs to the family room at the earliest they were allowed, 6:00 a.m., to open presents from under the tree. The boys received some clothes, which they were not thrilled with, but did like the basketball hoop and basketball, books, junior chemistry set, puzzles, board games, video games, and DVDs. Jeremy got some new music and a metronome, and Jordan got the best present ever —a cell phone —"to be used for emergencies when you're trail riding," Mrs. Chambers pointed out. They also got some candy and an orange in their stockings.

And, in true tradition, Banner and Penny got some treats in their stockings, too! From their grandparents, both boys received checks to deposit into their college savings plans. For some reason, these gifts seemed to excite their parents a lot more than Jordan and Jeremy.

Jordan had a hard time putting down his new cell phone, but eventually he got dressed and he, Jeremy, and their mom went out to the barn to give the horses their Christmas treats, before they got started on the normal chores. Jeremy slipped a couple extra carrots to both Penny and Banner, and Jordan gave Laddie a big rawhide bone to gnaw on. Their mom hand fed pieces of apples to Banner. The Chambers family spent most of the rest of the day snacking, playing their new games and admiring all the presents. Then, late in the afternoon they loaded up in the SUV to have Christmas dinner with Mrs. Chambers' sister's family. They ate an enormous dinner and played games with their cousins while the adults chatted.

All too soon, it was time to head for home. They drove by the Eastons on the way home, to drop off presents for Chip and Molly. Chip was getting a soccer ball, and Molly a plastic model horse that looked just like Midnight, to add to her model horse collection.

As they pulled into the driveway, Mr. and Mrs. Easton waved from the window. Chip and Molly were playing in the front yard, trying to build what looked like a snowman, but Jake kept knocking it down. Chip threw a snowball at Jake, who dodged it easily.

Both Chip and Molly were wearing new jackets, hats, and mittens. Molly showed off her red mittens and jacket to Mrs. Chambers, who commented on how nice they were. Chip listed all the presents he got, which included binoculars and also a cell phone. Jordan realized how handy the binoculars would be and wondered if Chip had asked for them or if it was purely coincidence.

While Molly chattered to the parents, Chip whispered to Jordan and Jeremy that he hadn't seen anything going on at Carson's house lately. The Chambers drove home, after Chip and Molly thanked them for the gifts.

The Chambers family arrived back at their farm, and quickly did the chores in the barn. Jordan and Jeremy were so tired they went right to bed, with smiles on their faces. It had been a great Christmas!

Chapter 6

More Wintertime Fun

On the Saturday morning after Christmas, Jeremy and Jordan awoke to a blanket of fluffy snow in their yard.

"It must've snowed all night," Jeremy yelled to Jordan as they both stared out Jordan's bedroom window. "Let's go horseback sledding!"

After finishing their chores in the barn in record time, they ate a quick breakfast, and then got ready for fun.

"Get back to your rooms and put some long johns on!" Mrs. Chambers barked when they told her what they planned to do.

Neither boy said a word as they headed back to their bedrooms. They knew she was stressed out from work and that it was wise to be quiet and do whatever she told them to do whenever she got behind in her work.

After putting on another layer of clothing, the boys ran back to the barn and saddled Banner, then led him outside the barn. They had their trusty sled waiting. First they tied a long, strong rope to the sled then Jordan scrambled up on Banner, while holding the end of it. He wrapped it loosely around the saddle horn. Banner, quite used to these games and to driving, waited patiently, and didn't mind the rope across his hindquarters.

Jeremy lay down on the sled and waited eagerly. Jordan moved Banner out at a walk at first. Once they got into the snow-covered field, he trotted until they came across a snowmobile track. The snowmobilers had been out last night, and made a handy web of trails in the large field.

Jordan glanced back once or twice to make sure Jeremy was still hanging on.

"Let 'er rip!" Jeremy yelled. So Jordan urged Banner to a lope. Banner knew this game well, and ran smoothly, towing the sled with Jeremy clinging on for dear life. Snow flew from Banner's churning hooves into Jeremy's face as he raced around the field. Jeremy was laughing and yelling as he slid all over the sled, but somehow managed to hang on.

"Banner's getting tired," Jordan said. "So, I guess it's time for a quick rest, then it's my turn!"

Jeremy enjoyed being able to ride Banner, for once. Much as he liked Penny, riding Banner was like riding a Cadillac. After falling off the sled a couple times, both of the boys ended up covered in snow and glad their mom yelled at them to put their long johns on under their jeans. Banner became tired, so they carefully cooled him down, before they unsaddled him and turned him back out in the pasture with Penny.

Cold, but happy, the boys trooped back into their warm house. Steaming mugs of hot cocoa soon warmed them up. They sat by the fireplace, enjoying a crackling fire. Looking at their rosy cheeks, Mrs. Chambers said enviously, "I sure wish I could have joined you. Looks like you had a lot of fun!"

Jordan warmed up by playing video games and of course, Jeremy practiced the piano then read a little. Later that afternoon, Chip and Molly came over and they all went back outside. It only took one snowball, thrown by Molly of all people, to launch a huge snowball fight. Molly and Jeremy got the worst of it, but did hold their ground for a few minutes at least.

They warmed up again inside the house, and then walked back to the barn together where Midnight and Rocket were ready to take Chip and

Molly back home. As they approached their horses, Jordan told them about the sledding fun he and Jeremy had that morning.

"Hey, let's have Banner take us out before we go home!" Chip said, as his cell phone rang. It was his mom. "Come on, Molly," Chip said as he ended the call, "Mom says we have to get right home!"

"Don't worry, Chip," Jordan said, "There's a whole lot more winter left. We'll get Banner to take you sledding real soon."

As they re-saddled a very furry Rocket, and feisty little Midnight, Chip gave his fellow detectives an update.

"There's been more comings and goings at Carson's place. I've seen a different car coming in almost every night. My binoculars were the best present ever!"

Jeremy spoke up, "Jordan's going to talk to Amanda at the next Riders meeting, and see if she can get her dad to run the license plate and arrest Mr. Carson. So keep watching. More evidence is better!"

New Year's Day came and went and soon the kids were back in the routine of school, chores and homework. Then it was time for the January Frolic Riders meeting. Since they wouldn't be meeting with their horses, it was a lot easier to get ready and go to the meeting, especially for Mrs. Chambers.

Right before they took off, Jordan crammed a copy of the letter they had written in his jeans pocket. When they got to the meeting, Chip and Molly were standing at the door waiting for them. Jordan showed the letter to Chip and Molly to prove that tonight was the night he was going to approach Amanda.

"I'll look for the right time for you to talk to her," Chip said.

"I'll know the right time, Chip. You just want an excuse to stare at her."

As everyone was still arriving, Jordan noticed Amanda was standing alone, staring down at a clip board she was holding. He slowly walked up to her.

"Excuse me, Amanda. Can I ask you something?"

"Sure, Jordan, if you're wondering when our next training practice is, I'm working on the schedule right now. I'll have it ready by the end of the meeting."

"Thanks. That was one thing I wanted to know. But actually, this is kind of like a favor."

Just then, out of the corner of his eye, Jordan noticed that Chip, Molly and Jeremy were standing right behind him, trying to listen.

"A favor? Well, maybe. What is it?" Amanda asked as Jordan reached in his back pocket for the letter.

"I want you to give this letter to your father. We sent it to the Frolicville Police but they haven't done anything," Jordan said as he slid his hand inside his pocket, which was empty! Just then, he remembered that Chip hadn't given him the letter back. Chip realized the same thing at the same time and quickly handed the letter to Amanda.

Unfortunately, some of the other Riders who were nearby saw the exchange and thought Chip was passing a love note to Amanda. They immediately started making kissing gestures to Chip. Chip rolled his eyes and faked a laugh, but was really embarrassed. If they only knew how close they were to being right.

Amanda just shrugged it off and took the letter.

"I'll read this later and let you know, OK? Now, we better take our seats. The meeting is gonna start any minute," she said as she clipped the letter to the back of the clipboard.

Chapter 7

A Cookie Sale and a Spring Horse Show

The rest of January was cold and routine. Off to school in the morning when it was still dark outside, then the bus ride home when the sun was starting to set, then dinner and homework and off to bed – with a little time in between for TV and video games (Chip and Jordan), piano practice (Jeremy) and reading books and newspapers (Jeremy and Molly).

All four kids were glad when it was time for the February Frolic Riders meeting. They could hardly wait to hear what Amanda had to tell them about the police investigation of Mr. Carson that her father was probably conducting.

Just like the January meeting, this meeting was without horses so shortly after dinner, Jordan and Jeremy loaded into the SUV and Mrs. Chambers drove them to the meeting. Mrs. Easton had done the same for Molly and Chip, who were waiting for the boys at the entrance.

"It's about time you got here!" Chip said as Jordan and Jeremy approached him. "Amanda isn't here yet! What if she doesn't come tonight? Then what'll we do?"

"Relax, Chip," Jordan said. "It's still early."

"OK, everyone. Time to get started," Mr. Grimmer yelled. "Oh, hello Amanda, how nice that you could join us," he said as Amanda rushed into the room with her jacket half off; her clipboard was stuffed under her left arm while she tried to carry a big box of catalogs and papers with just her right arm.

"Sorry I'm late," she said as she dropped the box and clipboard on the floor.

"She's probably late cuz' her dad was giving her up to the minute details of the police investigation," Chip whispered to Jordan.

Amanda tore off her jacket, picked up her clipboard from the floor and moved to the front of the room.

"Hi everybody. As you know, February is the month for our annual fundraising cookie sale. Remember, this is to make sure we have a great spring show and super fun spring camping trip this year! I have cookie brochures, order forms and a map for each of you showing you your sales territory. Our goal is to double our sales from last year so everyone please put forth an extra effort to sell at least two boxes of cookies to every customer on your list. And now, we're going to watch a video produced by the Coco Cookies Company that will help all of us know everything there is to know about these cookies."

"I'd rather watch paint dry," Chip said rather loudly as the video began.

Right then, about six other kids and a couple parents looked at Chip and yelled, "Sshhhhhh!"

Chip straightened up and pretended to watch the video with great interest, which was not as hard as he thought. Each time a new cookie was shown, he kept wondering if that would be the one that would end up being his favorite.

After the video, a mad flurry of kids rushed up to Amanda to get their brochures, order forms and territory maps. Chip, Jordan, Jeremy and

Molly looked at each other with the same expression that said, "Jordan's never going to be able to talk to her tonight."

As they silently waited in the chaotic line to get their cookie sales supplies, Jordan finally said, "We'll just keep doin' what we've been doin'. Chip, you're on surveillance, Molly and Jeremy, keep reading the papers, tear out stories about car thefts and put 'em in your scrapbook, and I'll stay on the vaulting team.

"We won't get a chance to talk to Amanda at the regular March meeting. It'll be as nuts as this one since it's when we pick up the cookies we sold. But, I have her phone number and I could call her and ask her something about the spring horse show next month and what I'm supposed to do for the vaulting team. And besides, even if I don't call her, after reading our letter, the police are probably on the case and making a lot more progress than we are."

"Good thinkin', Jordan," Jeremy said.

Eventually, each of the four kids got their cookie sales supplies. When Chip saw his and Molly's territory map, he was so excited he let out a big "Yahoo!" It was the first year he and Molly were going to be allowed to deliver cookies by themselves, without their mom driving them and he had a plan for how he and Molly would deliver the cookies they sold. As soon as he saw their sales territory, he knew his plan would work!

As February got closer to March, the days got a wee bit warmer, the sun shone a wee bit brighter and the days got a wee bit longer. All of these things added together meant that Jordan and Jeremy were able to spend more time outside with their horses, or up in the tree house.

Chip spent his extra outdoors time pretending to groom Rocket while keeping an eye on Mr. Carson's property. Peering through his binoculars, he dictated each new car and its description that he saw on the property into a digital recorder, which he was supposed to be using for recording classroom lectures to improve his grades. Then, he would sneak into Molly's room and give her the recorder.

"Here's tonight's intel," Chip would say as he handed Molly the recorder.

Molly would listen and then try to write down what Chip had recorded. Chip often talked too fast or too much, so Molly decided the most important thing to write was the date, the kind of car and its color. Then, she put the report in the scrapbook she and Jeremy were compiling.

One night in early March, shortly after receiving the recorder from Chip, Molly asked, "How do you spell Bamero, Chip?"

"It's Camaro, Ca-CA-CA, Ca-ma-ro, so it probably starts with a K or a C." Chip replied, "Just write it like it sounds, Jeremy will correct it if it's wrong. He's the best speller."

For the next week, Chip only saw Jordan in school because he and Jeremy were grounded for accidentally breaking their mom's favorite vase while wrestling over the TV remote, spending more than the allotted time on video games (Jordan), and both not cleaning their rooms when asked. Despite being grounded, the boys were still allowed to ride on their own property, and they were allowed to go out to sell cookies to neighbors, under their mom's supervision, of course. But, they were not allowed to have any friends come over, which really meant, no Chip and Molly.

The time did pass, and before they knew it, it was time for the March meeting – which was when the Riders picked up the boxes of cookies they sold so they could be delivered. Amanda began the meeting by announcing that they were only one case short of their sales goal, then added, "Congratulations, everybody – and thanks!"

As Jordan predicted, things were chaotic, but eventually everybody got the right amount and types of cookies they had sold.

As everyone was loading their cookies into their cars, Amanda yelled, "And remember Riders – practice, practice, practice! The spring horse show will be here before you know it!"

After school the next day, Chip and Molly and Jordan and Jeremy rushed through their homework and an early dinner. It was cookie delivery night and they were anxious to get started. Chip was finally able to try out his great idea. When he told Molly about it, she was so excited she wanted to leave right then and there.

"Not so fast, Molly, our horses have to look perfect, so first we have to groom Midnight and Rocket, including cleaning and polishing their tack," Chip said calmly.

"OK! OK! Let's get out to the barn," Molly said flying out of the house.

"There you go again, Molly. Hang on! You have to help me carry the cookies out!"

It took a couple trips but the two eventually got all the boxes of cookies neatly stacked up next to the horses. After one more inspection to make sure Rocket and Midnight looked good, Chip put a big saddlebag behind his saddle on Rocket, and filled it with the boxes of cookies. Then, they went back in the house and changed into their Rider uniforms. Chip put the order list and a pen in his pocket, and they were ready to ride.

Molly rode Midnight closely beside Chip and Rocket. As they rode up to each house, Molly jumped off Midnight and handed the reins to Chip, who handed her the cookies. Molly delivered the cookies, and collected the payment, which was always a check. Once Molly was back in her saddle, Chip checked the name off the list and carefully pocketed the check.

This was the first year Chip and Molly were allowed to go out on their own. In past years, their mom drove them in the car, and kept track of the checks and cookies. This new method did involve some cookie breakage, but the customers enjoyed it just the same. Some of the people took pictures, and some posed their own children with the young Riders on horseback. Some of the youngest kids even sat on Midnight, with Molly's permission.

The Chambers, on the other hand, made cookie delivery a family affair, and everyone but Penny got to join in. The boys carefully groomed Banner, and adorned his harness with bells, then Mrs. Chambers hitched him to their buggy. With little to no snow, they couldn't use the sleigh. The buggy was a shiny black, four-wheeled cart with a red fringed top.

It could seat four comfortably, two people on each seat. After helping the boys load the cookies, Mr. and Mrs. Chambers shared one seat, and the boys, dressed in their full Junior Rider uniforms, shared the other.

As they arrived at each driveway, the boys took turns running up to the house with the boxes of cookies. All the stops had been prearranged by Jordan, who had spent a lot of time on the phone setting up the appointments. The families were thrilled with the photo opportunity, especially when they had little kids, who got to sit in the buggy with them to pose for pictures. They covered several miles, and delivered over one hundred boxes of cookies.

After the excitement of delivering the cookies, all four kids settled into getting ready for the spring horse show, which was only three weeks away. Jordan and Jeremy practiced their riding techniques, and their mom gave them lessons every day in their sandy riding ring. Molly and Chip rode over frequently, to get in some lesson and practice time as well.

As the day neared, in addition to practicing, they cleaned all their equipment, and polished their boots. Jordan's dress uniform had become too small, so Jeremy got it, and Jordan got a brand new one. Both boys got new black helmets, so Jordan gave his old one to Chip because it was in better shape than the one he had. Chip was still able to fit into his uniform, but the pants seemed a little shorter than he remembered. Tucked into his new boots, he figured no one would notice.

Before they knew it, it was the last Saturday in March – the day of the spring horse show.

Jordan and Jeremy felt butterflies in their stomachs as they loaded up Banner and Penny for the haul to the show grounds. The morning classes were devoted to the western and English pleasure events, along with fitting and showing halter classes for each age level. Jordan and Banner took first place in their class, mostly because Banner was an old pro at horse shows and knew how to pose well. He stood like a statue, while Penny fussed a little and moved her feet out of position. Jeremy didn't place, but received his merit badge anyway for a job well done.

Molly and Midnight did very well in their class, and took home a third place ribbon, even though Midnight kept swishing his tail and stomping his hooves, and didn't trot very willingly. But, it was fine with Molly, she was happy to receive her merit badge too.

Chip and Rocket did not fare so well. Rocket wasn't much of a show horse, and showed his boredom by pawing impatiently, and sending clouds of dust all over Chip's polished boots. When the judge came by to inspect them, Rocket turned impatiently and accidentally stepped on Chip's foot. Chip did not get his merit badge in showmanship. He scowled at Rocket, who just looked at him innocently.

They all entered western pleasure, and once again, Banner came out on top. Penny was a little speedy with her lope, but Jeremy kept her under control. They collected a sixth place ribbon, and both boys received merit badges. Chip and Rocket had a few problems, but managed to get the merit badge somehow. Molly and Midnight did very well in the Cadet class, and won second place and a merit badge.

The classes in the afternoon consisted of the gymkhana events, such as the barrel race, pole bending, keyhole, flag race, and an exciting reining event for the most advanced Riders.

"I bet Banner could do reining," exclaimed Jordan, who had boundless faith in his loyal steed.

His mom replied, "Maybe in his younger days, but I don't want to risk a bowed tendon. We'll sit this one out."

Jordan was disappointed, but stayed on the rail to watch Penny and Jeremy compete. Penny easily won the barrel race, just as she had last fall. She and Jeremy also won the keyhole event, because she was so nimble and quick with her turns. They came in a close second on the flag race, too. Jeremy was so proud to collect two blue ribbons, and a red for the second place.

Chip and Rocket were fast, but didn't turn so efficiently. Rocket ran wide around the barrels, but still managed to get a third place and yellow ribbon for their efforts. Molly and Midnight did well in the keyhole event and flag race, and won second and third place ribbons in those events. Most of the other ponies didn't handle as smoothly for their young riders.

Then it was time to line up on the rail to watch the reining event for the Senior Riders. When Amanda finished her run, the boys whispered to each other that they had to find a way to talk to her. It had been months since she got the letter and they needed to know what was going on!

"What we need is a diversion," Jeremy said.

"I know," Molly piped up. "Come with me, Jeremy, and we'll distract our folks while Chip and Jordan go over to Amanda's horse trailer and see if she talked to her dad."

They all agreed, and split up.

Jeremy and Molly distracted their parents by pointing out a potentially sore leg on Penny. As expected, the parents all crowded around the small mare to examine her leg. Jordan and Chip walked quickly over to Amanda's trailer. Jordan told her how great her reining demonstration was, while Chip stood nervously by. He couldn't seem to talk. Amanda thanked Jordan, while unsaddling her horse.

"What did your dad do about the letter Chip and I gave you?"

"What letter?" Amanda asked.

"What letter? What d'ya mean what letter?" Jordan exclaimed. "The letter we gave you at the end of the January meeting, about Chip's neighbor, Mr. Carson, running a chop shop with stolen cars and everything. We found a license plate in Skeleton Creek and put the number in the letter for the police to check. We want your dad to check it out and arrest him! Could you get him to go over there?" Jordan blurted out.

Chip still just stood there. He opened his mouth, but nothing was coming out.

Amanda said, "Wow. I'm sorry. I must have wadded the letter up in my pocket and forgot about it. Anyway, how can you be so sure he's running a chop shop?"

"Chip has been keeping an eye on Mr. Carson's place since last summer and keeps seeing different cars being driven in, other cars being driven out, and sometimes flatbed trucks carry stripped cars out. My brother Jeremy and Chip's sister Molly have been keeping track of every car Chip has seen over there and they put together a scrapbook of newspaper stories about people getting their cars stolen and about stolen cars being used in robberies and stuff. I saw some sports cars there myself." Jordan clarified.

"Well, even if I did read the letter you wrote, I wouldn't have shown it to my dad without proof. Do you have any pictures of the stolen cars, or anything else?" She asked.

"No, but we can get some!" Jordan blurted out without thinking.

"Well, take some good pictures. Then bring them to me and I'll show them to my dad. Make sure you give me the license plate number when you give me the pictures. I'll ask my dad to run the plate then, too. They call that a LEIN check," she added.

"Ok," agreed Jordan. "Bye." Amanda smiled at both boys, and turned back to her horse.

Jordan and Chip quickly went to join their parents who were motioning to them to come back.

As they were walking away, Jordan realized Chip hadn't said a word. "Why didn't you say anything? You usually never shut up." Jordan asked.

"Amanda is so nice." Chip said.

"Now you can talk, and that's all you can say? That she's nice! She didn't even give her dad the letter!" Jordan complained.

"She's really pretty, too!" Chip said.

"Oh forget it! It's a good thing I'm on Amanda detail." Jordan huffed.

On the way home, both Jordan and Jeremy were so tired, they nearly fell asleep. Once they arrived back home, there were still chores to be done – the horses and tack had to be unloaded and put away. Mr. and Mrs. Chambers helped with the feeding and watering so the two sweaty, grimy boys could take showers before going to bed. Usually they fussed and argued about having to take a shower or go to bed early, but that night they were too tired to complain, and fell into bed exhausted.

Two days later, the four of them were on horseback, as usual, in the riding ring at the Chambers' farm. Before they started riding and playing, they discussed the latest developments.

"So you see," Jordan said, "We've got to get a good digital camera so we can get decent pictures of some of the stolen cars."

"Doesn't your mom have a digital camera?" Chip asked.

"Yes, but she'd kill us if we used it without permission. Besides, we don't even know how to use one." Jeremy explained.

Chip said reluctantly, "Well, I guess I could ask for one for my birthday. It's only a week away. I was going to ask for a new Rider uniform."

"Good idea!" Molly said brightly. "Besides, you can still fit into those pants; they're just a little short. We can practice with the camera too and, we can take it on the spring camping trip. It's only about four weeks away!" Molly said, barely containing her excitement. It would be her first Riders camping trip.

With that, they broke into a game they often played when they just wanted to have fun. Pretending to be cowboys, they set up a practice calf dummy and tried to rope it, but as usual, they weren't having much luck. Rocket and Midnight didn't care to have a rope whizzing past their heads, and kept shying away. Jordan finally managed to rope the dummy from a standstill. But it was Jeremy who seemed to get the hang of it.

He and Penny rode toward the dummy at a dead run, and Jeremy flipped the loop over the dummy. Penny stopped sharply and backed up to draw the rope tight, as they had practiced.

Molly clapped.

"Good job, Jeremy!" Jordan called out.

"I guess you've been practicing more than the piano!" Chip added.

"Thanks," Jeremy said.

Changing the subject, Chip said, "You guys ready for the camping trip?"

"Oh, yeah! We've got all our stuff ready to pack. It's going to be awesome." Jeremy exclaimed.

"It sure is. It's way more fun than the shows!" Jordan said.

"Who doesn't know that?" Chip asked as he took another shot at roping the practice dummy.

Chapter 8

Spring Camping Trip
Adventures

The following Friday, Chip woke up especially happy. It was his 12th birthday. But, just as he started thinking about the presents and cake he would get, he also told himself to be on guard for what else was probably in store for him. You see, Chip was born on April 1st – April Fool's Day, so he always got a few gag gifts and tricks pulled on him. For some reason, every year, he just didn't see it coming. "Not this year," Chip thought as he got out of bed. "Nobody's pulling anything on me."

"Happy Birthday, son," Mr. and Mrs. Easton said to Chip as he sat down for breakfast. "Chip, this is almost as special for me as it is for you. It's not often I'm home on your actual birthday, and I couldn't wait to give you your big present until tonight, so we'd like to give it to you now," Mr. Easton said, smiling, as he rose from the table to get Chip's gift.

He came back in the kitchen with a small box, wrapped in paper decorated with all sorts of rope knots. "Cool paper," Chip said as he tore it to shreds.

Inside was exactly what Chip had asked for. "Awesome! A digital camera! Thanks Mom! Thanks Dad!" Chip stared at the box and thought about all the pictures he would take of Mr. Carson's chop shop. He couldn't wait to tell Jordan and Jeremy.

As they rode the bus to school, Chip went on and on about his camera. Finally, when he stopped talking, Jordan handed him a pink envelope with that looked like a birthday card inside. "Here," Jordan said, "Amanda handed this to me last night at vaulting practice."

"Wow! Thanks! A card from Amanda!" Chip tore open the envelope and pulled out an index card. Then he read it: "April Fools! And Happy Birthday." It was signed, "Jeremy and Jordan".

"Very funny, thanks anyway," Chip said as he stuffed the card in his backpack.

Throughout the rest of April, when the boys weren't taking pictures of just about everything they saw, they were planning for the spring camping trip, which took place the first weekend in May. This was the first year since they'd been going on the camping trip that they didn't find it too hard to count down the days until one of their favorite weekends of the year, mostly because of their determination to prove that Mr. Carson was a criminal.

They spent just about every free minute they had together taking pictures with Chip's camera. They would ride to the edge of Carson's property, stand on stumps and rocks or anything that would make them tall enough to get the camera over the fence, and shoot from every angle they could get to without drawing attention to themselves.

A couple days before the camping trip, after taking three more pictures of the exact same thing – a black Jeep with the hood removed that was sitting in Carson's driveway – Chip turned to Jordan and said, "We'll have lots of evidence to tell Amanda about this weekend when we see her. She's coming on the camping trip, right, Jordan?"

"Chip, I must've told you a million times – YES!, she's coming! She's an Elite Rider so of course she'll be there and at some point, we'll be able to catch her alone long enough to tell her we'll have pictures for her! But, that's not the reason I'm going on the camping trip – I want to have fun! So stop worrying and start packing!" Jordan said as he crawled away from Carson's fence to get back on Banner.

Chip had to admit that Jordan had a point. After a long, cold winter, Chip, like every Frolic Rider, loved everything about the spring camping trip. Especially staying in tents, campers or, for those who had them, the living quarters in their horse trailers.

The policies were very strict; exceptions were never made. Each Cadet and Junior Rider had to be accompanied by at least one parent. The Cadets could camp and participate in a lot of the activities, but they could not bring or ride their horses or ponies on this trip. Junior Riders were allowed to bring and ride their horses on the organized trail ride, but only if they had at least the first level horsemanship merit badge.

In the evening, everyone – kids and parents – gathered around a campfire to toast marshmallows (which were a crowd favorite), swap stories (but no ghost stories until the Cadets and Junior Riders went to sleep), and sing camp songs, which were usually accompanied by someone who brought a guitar.

At last, the day had come! The Eastons and Chambers both arrived a few minutes after sunrise. They were all thankful that the sun was shining and the sky was pure blue and there was only a hint of a breeze. Without saying a word, Jordan, Jeremy and their mom knew to set up camp right next to Chip, Molly and Mrs. Easton.

After their cars were unpacked, they put the tents up, tethered the horses to long ropes and gave them lots of hay to munch on. Then, the boys' next chore was to go and get water for the horses. As they walked toward the pump, they passed by Amanda, who was busy setting up her campsite.

"We've got a digital camera and we're taking a bunch of pictures, Amanda." Jordan whispered.

Amanda smiled and said, "That's great, Jordan. Just bring 'em to me and I'll talk to my dad some more about it. He hasn't been too convinced yet."

Chip nodded his head but couldn't manage to utter a word as his eyes met hers.

Jordan stepped in front of Chip so he would stop staring at Amanda and said, "Thanks, Amanda! We won't let you down. See ya 'round. Now, come on, Chip, let's go get that water."

As the three boys walked back to their campsite, each carrying a heavy water bucket, they wobbled a bit and moved rather slowly. Jeremy had to stop to rest, but Jordan carried his bucket all the way to their campsite without spilling any. Chip, on the other hand, sloshed ice cold water all over his jeans and boots. His mom made him change his pants, and hang them on a line they had strung between the trees.

As a couple Senior Riders walked by, Chip heard them call out, "Hey, Chip – wet your pants already? It's not even dark out!"

"Ha, ha, really funny!" Chip yelled back from inside his tent as he put another pair of jeans on.

Then, Chip, Molly, and their mom joined forces with the Chambers family for a hearty breakfast. Together, they ate a delicious cheesy egg and sausage casserole that they cooked over their campfire in a Dutch oven.

As he was gulping down his last bite, Jordan said, "I wish Dad could have come too. He would love this."

"You know how his allergies are," Mrs. Chambers replied. "He'd be sneezing and coughing the whole time. Besides, someone needed to stay home to take care of Laddie and the cats." She replied.

Molly chimed in, "Our dad is home this weekend too, feeding Jake and Midnight for us. I don't think he wanted to come camping anyway. He gets awful tired, especially when he's on the road all week. I wish he'd get a job that would let him be home every night."

Mrs. Easton promptly said, "Now, Molly. We're lucky Dad has a good job. We shouldn't complain." Then she quickly herded her two children away to their campsite to tidy up before they left for the trail ride.

The Seniors had already left on their ride along the more challenging trails. As the next group got ready to ride off, the Cadets were instructed to observe the preparations. After the Junior Riders left, the Cadets had a grooming demonstration, practiced tying knots, and listened to some safety tips. If they behaved well, and had achieved their first level horsemanship badge, they would be allowed to bring their ponies on the next camping trip. Molly paid close attention, and was determined that she and Midnight would qualify next time. She'd had enough of hanging around the "little kids".

After a couple hours, Jordan, Jeremy, and Chip returned from the morning trail ride. They unsaddled and rubbed down their horses before they sat down to a lunch of thick ham and cheese sandwiches, chips, veggies and dip, and apple slices. They ate quickly; after lunch, it was time to go to the lake and swim.

Once everyone was done eating and lunch dishes and trash had been cleaned up, the Junior Riders walked together down a gravel road next to the woods toward the small lake. Molly started out with the other Cadets, but found them boring. She hustled ahead to walk with her brother and his friends. Jeremy smiled at her, letting her know it was OK for her to join them, when she appeared by his side.

Chip immediately started talking in a loud Frankenstein kind of voice about the big snakes in the deepest part of the woods, and the giant spiders. "Black widow spiders, you know. They'll kill you if they bite you," he said as Molly and Jeremy both shivered at the thought.

Once the Riders all reached the lake, they quickly discovered just how cold the water was so only a few of the bravest ones actually swam. The adult leaders and most of the children just waded along the shore, picking up stones and shells. The beach was sandy, and great for playing tag and making sandcastles. Jordan, Jeremy, Chip, and Molly worked hard on making a particularly impressive sandcastle, complete with a moat and twig drawbridge.

They took the opportunity to discuss their next steps in the Skeleton Creek caper.

"We've got a bunch of pictures, but how are we gonna get them to Amanda? I can't give her my camera! I don't have her email or anything, and besides, I don't even know how to download them, yet." Chip complained.

"Can't you just print them out?" Jeremy asked.

"No. I can't be alone on our computer long enough. It would take a long time – not to mention all the photo paper and ink. My parents would be suspicious. They'd find out what I'm doing."

All four kids went quiet. As they thought about what to do, they each tossed sand around with their hands. Finally Jordan broke the silence.

"How about this? What if we pool our money together and buy a box of photo paper and color ink for your printer? Then, Chip, somehow we'll figure out a way for all of us to get on your computer long enough to print them out. Your mom will think we're doing homework or playing a game. Or, maybe you can do it one night during the week...no, forget that! It will take all four of us to pull this off to make sure we don't make any mistakes, like forgetting to take out the ink cartridges and paper from the printer and put in our stuff BEFORE we start printing the pictures! Then, put the other ones back when we're done."

"Great thinking, Jordan!" Jeremy exclaimed. "Chip, how much money have you got?"

"Uh, I kinda' spent all my money on candy and stuff for this camping trip."

"Well," Jordan said, "Jeremy and I both have money in our "Grow" and "Get" jars. I'm not sure, but I bet we'll need at least $20.00 or $30.00 for ink and paper. Jeremy, how much do you think you have?"

"I have $53 in my "Grow" jar and $7 in my "Get" jar. Jordan, you know we can't use any money from our "Give" jars – that's for church and stuff."

"I know, I know!" Jordan said, then added, "OK, so you have $60 and I have $42 – without counting my "Give" money. So, I'm pretty sure we have enough."

"Wait a minute," Chip said. "How come you guys have so much money?"

"Because, Chip," Jeremy said, "whenever we get or earn money, we divide it up in our three jars. You've seen them – don't you remember? Anyway, when we buy candy and stuff, we can only use money from our "Get" jar. Our "Give" jar is for charities and needy people; we usually take that money to church. Our "Grow" jar is for saving up for something special or an emergency. Jordan, this counts as an emergency, right?"

"Yeah, I'd say so."

"Wow!" Chip said. "I gotta' get me some of those jars! We couldn't pull off the Skeleton Creek caper without 'em."

"OK. So we have a plan and we have the money. Now we gotta' figure out a way to get to a store to buy the stuff and get on your computer long enough to print out the pictures without getting caught."

"I know. Next Saturday, we can ride our horses to OK Office Supplies store. They have tons of printer stuff. We'll just tell our parents we're going on a trail ride; it won't be a lie 'cuz we really will be riding trails!" Chip said, happy to contribute to the plan.

"OK, let me think," Jordan said. "That sounds like it will work. We don't have anything else to do next Saturday, so I don't know why we couldn't get permission to go for a ride."

Jordan paused for a minute, the other kids got real quiet, ready to hear whatever he said next. Finally, Jordan spoke.

"One other thing, we have to be extra good this week; we can't do anything that will get any one of us grounded!"

"Good thinkin'," Molly chimed in.

"It's harder than it sounds," Chip said. "But, it's for a good cause!"

Jordan continued. "OK, so let's say we get the ink and paper and we're able to print out the pictures. The next step is to get them to Amanda. Hmmmmm...."

"I know!" Jeremy chimed in. "You can give 'em to Amanda at your next vaulting practice. Isn't it in about two weeks?"

"That's it!" Jordan said.

"Perfecto!" Chip said as he, Jordan, Jeremy and even Molly, high-fived each other.

The four detectives stood up and started brushing sand off their legs and arms when they heard their names being called. It was time to head back to their campsites. They noticed some of the Senior Riders were already walking back on a trail through the forest and some of Junior Riders had taken off walking along a dirt path that skirted the lake. Molly saw that the Cadets were being led by some of the parents along the main road.

"Come on, let's catch up with our buddies on the dirt path," Jordan said.

All three boys started running at the same time. But Molly stood still and yelled out to them, "I'm gonna catch up to the Cadets." Then she ran over to the trail that the Senior Riders were on.

The boys thought the walk along the dirt path took a long time, but eventually, they arrived back at the camp. Jordan and Jeremy were surprised that Banner and Penny seemed tired and sweaty. It turned out that while they were at the lake, some of the parents went for a trail ride. Mrs. Easton had wisely chosen to ride Penny, who was a better-trained horse for an inexperienced rider. Mrs. Chambers enjoyed a nice ride on her beloved horse Banner. The boys helped unsaddle the horses, and then cool them down. They were relieved that Molly was with the Cadets; it was a nice break for them.

But, while Molly told them she was taking a shortcut to catch up to the other Cadets, she was really trying to beat Chip back to the camp, so she could have a ride on Rocket while Chip wasn't around. Molly started on the same trail as the Senior Riders, but soon lost sight of them around a bend. She came to a fork in the trail, and took the one she was sure would take her right back to camp, much faster than the gravel road. Soon, the forest was so thick she could barely see the trail. She decided to speed up to get back to camp quicker.

Molly didn't realize it, but she was headed in exactly the wrong direction, away from camp, and into the roughest trails in the park. Molly thought about the big spiders and huge black snakes Chip had warned her about, and swallowed hard. She told herself she wouldn't cry though. "Cadets don't cry," Molly said to herself.

Meanwhile, back at the camp, pandemonium broke out when Molly failed to show up with the other Cadets. Her mom was beside herself when all the other Cadets and Junior Riders were accounted for. The Seniors had already ridden off again to take one last short trail ride. Mrs. Easton asked Chip, Jordan, and Jeremy what happened.

Chip told her, "Molly was walking with us, but all of a sudden she said was going to catch up with the Cadets, but I kind of figured she was gonna follow the Senior Riders."

A twinge of guilt crept into Chip's face, which was several shades paler now. He was her big brother, after all, and should have looked after her. She was only eight years old.

"Darn that Molly," he whispered to Jordan. "She always has to be so independent and go off on her own. I wish she'd settle down and act normal."

The parents prepared to go off in search of Molly. They took their cell phones, a first aid kit, Molly's sweatshirt, canteens, ponchos, flashlights, and a blanket. Mr. Grimmer was saddled and ready to go with the moms. Mrs. Chambers swung up on Banner, and Mrs. Easton mounted Penny.

Chip asked both moms, "Can I come too? I can ride Rocket. He's fresher than Banner and Penny, and Molly can ride double with me on the way back. Besides, I can point out exactly where she left our group." Chip was persuasive, his mom nodded yes and he quickly mounted Rocket.

"Molly will ride home with me on Banner," Mrs. Chambers said. Then, just as she was ready to ride away, Jeremy walked up to Banner and whispered to him, "Find her, boy. She's just little and will be scared. I know you can do it!"

"Stay put, you two!" Mrs. Chambers hollered out to Jordan and Jeremy. "You call me on my cell phone immediately if Molly turns up back here."

"I'll keep my eye on everyone here," Amanda, who had decided not to go on the final trail ride, called out. Too worried about Molly to complain about having Amanda as a babysitter, Jordan and Jeremy waved good-bye to the parents as they left in search of their friend.

They needed to find Molly before dark, which would be in just a few hours. The temperature seemed to be dropping, and storm clouds were rolling in.

Meanwhile, Molly was so tired from wandering on the trails that she finally found a handy log near the path, and after checking carefully for spiders and snakes, she sat down to wait. She remembered from some of the safety classes that she was supposed to stay where she was, and let the searchers find her. She hollered for help until she was hoarse. She looked anxiously up and down the trail, and listened hard for any rescuers.

It was getting cold, and Molly shivered. She wrapped her little arms around her legs for warmth, and huddled on the log for what seemed like hours. Nighttime was closing in. Molly dozed off for a minute, then jerked awake. Did she hear the sound of hoof beats?

The searchers, meanwhile, were almost at their wits' end. Where could Molly be? They had ridden for almost two hours, and covered all the regularly-used trails in the park, to no avail. There was no sign of Molly. Mrs. Chambers called Jordan on his cell phone to see if Molly arrived back at camp. Sadly, she hadn't.

Everyone's voice was almost gone from calling out to Molly; Chip was so hoarse he started whistling through his fingers every few minutes. Just when they were starting to feel desperate, with darkness closing in and a chill brewing in the air, they came to a fork in the trail. Banner, for some reason, started down the left trail that led away from the campgrounds. It was little-used because it was rocky and swampy in spots.

Banner seemed determined, though, so Mrs. Chambers said, "Well, Banner wants to try this trail. Maybe he knows something we don't. This is one trail we haven't covered yet."

She let the horse choose their path, and he started to jog, almost as if he realized the urgency of their mission. Chip smiled grimly, and patted Rocket on the neck.

"Let's hope Banner knows what he's doing," Chip whispered to Rocket.

The searchers were surprised at the brisk pace Banner set, in spite of the rocks. All of the horses picked their way through efficiently. They came to a very muddy area, and looked carefully for any Molly-sized footprints, with no luck.

"Ya' know," Chip pointed out, "she could have walked on some of the logs at the side of the trail, and not left any footprints."

The adults agreed, and they continued on. Banner's ears were pricked forward, and he plowed on, right through the mud hole. Mrs. Chambers was surprised, because Banner didn't usually like to get his feet muddy. Penny followed loyally right behind.

Mr. Grimmer had trouble with his big gelding, which absolutely refused to go through the mud. He took off through the thick brush at the side of the trail. Chip winced as he saw the picker bushes attack both man and horse. Rocket looked first at the mud hole, then at Mr. Grimmer's big bay gelding, Pilot, who was struggling through the brush. Neither option appealed to Rocket, who hated being left behind. Rocket gathered himself and took a mighty leap, completely clearing the mud hole.

Unfortunately, Chip wasn't quite so lucky. He tumbled off Rocket about midway over the deepest part of the mud hole. Chip landed with a splash in the center of the hole, in a seated position. Mud flew everywhere.

Banner and Penny stopped quickly, and turned around at the sound of the big splash. As Rocket raced by, Mrs. Chambers reached out and grabbed his reins so he wouldn't get away. After seeing that Chip was alright, she commented to Chip's mom, "Now you know why I suggested you ride Penny."

Chip was so wet and dirty that he actually had to wring out his jacket. He sat down on a log to empty his new boots of mud and debris. His mom handed him Molly's sweatshirt to wear, which was pink with a little mermaid on it and way too small. But, he squeezed into it anyway. Chip wasn't physically hurt, but he sure was embarrassed.

Fortunately, Rocket was also fine and entirely too proud of himself. Chip noticed a suspicious gleam in Rocket's eyes, and had the distinct feeling that his horse was laughing at him. Muttering under his breath, Chip mounted up.

Mr. Grimmer, whose jacket was torn, and hands and face scratched from the brambles, joined them and they continued on the rough trail. Chip whispered to Rocket that he could forget about any carrot treats for the next week.

Everyone continued to take turns calling Molly's name. Chip kept whistling. Mr. Grimmer blew a loud whistle, but his horse spooked and he almost fell off. Chip noticed that Mr. Grimmer's face looked kind of tight and angry. His mom just looked sad and worried.

All of a sudden, Banner perked up his ears and looked intently down the trail. "I think Banner sees something ahead!" Mrs. Chambers said hopefully.

With no urging, Banner quickened his pace to a trot again. They rounded a bend and saw a bunch of branches laid carefully across the trail, in the shape of a giant arrow. When he came close to it, Banner stopped abruptly, as did the horses following his lead. A grimy little girl was sound asleep, sitting on a log with her back against a tall tree. Banner snorted, which almost sounded like a laugh and Molly woke up with a start. Joyfully, she ran to her mom, who jumped off Penny, and gathered her little girl tight in her arms.

They all dismounted and hugged her – relieved and grateful that she was alright. Molly grinned when she saw how filthy Chip was, and that he was squeezed into her Little Mermaid sweatshirt. She knew better than to say a word.

"It was Banner who found you, you know," Chip said.

Molly stroked Banner's neck, and he put his face near hers. She kissed him on the end of his nose. He almost seemed to be smiling.

Molly appeared to be fine. Mrs. Easton wrapped her up in a blanket and Mr. Grimmer mounted her behind Mrs. Chambers on Banner for the ride back to camp. The trip back to camp was uneventful, with Banner's unerring sense of direction. When they reached the mud hole, Chip dismounted and led Rocket around it.

Mr. Grimmer unfortunately took another trip through the picker bushes. Molly noticed that, as usual, he was not in the best of moods. She realized she would not be getting any merit badges on this camping trip, and seriously doubted that she would be allowed to bring Midnight for the next camping trip.

When they arrived back at camp, the Cadets and Riders, who were roasting hot dogs on the campfire for the cold, tired and hungry rescuers, cheered to see them all safe and sound. The rescuers put their horses up for a well-deserved rest. Jeremy's and Jordan's eyes opened wide when they saw how filthy Chip looked. They quickly began to rub down Banner and Penny while trying hard not to laugh at Chip, who certainly looked a mess.

"Nice shirt," Jordan commented.

Chip looked down and realized he was still wearing Molly's pink sweatshirt. He quickly tugged it off, and trotted over to his own campsite to find his duffel bag with a spare shirt to wear.

It was a quiet campfire scene that night. After eating hot dogs, they roasted marshmallows. A few stories were told and Amanda played a couple songs on her guitar. But, the scare that Molly gave everyone took its toll and the kids and parents all went to sleep very early.

The next morning, as the sun peeked out, the campers began taking their tents down. The horses were fed and watered, and then loaded in their trailers. Once the cars and horses were all packed up, the families headed for home.

Jordan and Jeremy were totally wiped out and didn't squabble once. Chip and Molly were so exhausted from their ordeal, that they both fell sound asleep almost immediately and didn't wake up until their mom told them they were home.

Chapter 9
Saturday Sleuthing

Throughout the next week, all four kids concentrated on being on their best behavior. They didn't argue over whose turn it was to set the table, clear the table, or wash the dishes. Mrs. Easton and Mrs. Chambers were quite amazed to see their kids actually working together on household chores. There had never been a problem with them taking care of their horses, but that never carried over to things like taking out the trash, or cleaning the garage.

On Wednesday after school, Jeremy volunteered to ride home on the bus with Molly and help her with her math homework. Mrs. Chambers had driven to the Eastons to pick him up and Jordan decided to ride along. On the way home, realizing that their plan was working brilliantly, Jordan asked his mom if they could go on a trail ride Saturday morning.

"Where are you planning to ride?" She asked.

"Chip and Molly will come too, so we'll just ride on the trails, and maybe over to Mill Road."

Mill Road would eventually lead to OK Office Supplies but Jordan left out this bit of information. "We'll take a lunch and make a nice trip. We might be gone a few hours, okay?"

"Please, Mom?" Jeremy added with an over- sweet, innocent smile that should have tipped her off. But, she was so proud of him helping Molly with her homework that she couldn't refuse.

"Well, ok, but be back by 2 or 3. And, don't run Banner at all, it might be too hard on him. Just walk, jog, and lope a little. And be careful, especially if Molly goes along."

Jeremy piped up, "We'll always take care of Molly."

Once they got on the bus the next day, they confirmed with Chip that he was allowed to go, but Molly wouldn't be able to, due to last weekend's escapade. "She even cried, but Mom wouldn't budge," Chip reported. "We'll have to go without her."

"Oh well, that' s OK. One less thing to worry about. Besides, we'll need her at your house way more than on the trail ride."

Saturday morning finally came. It dawned clear and warm, but not hot. The boys did their chores in record time, packed their lunches, and were saddled and ready to go by 10 a.m. Jordan called Chip, who told him he was ready to go. Jordan could hear a disappointed Molly in the background.

"I'll have Rocket saddled by the time you get here," Chip declared.

Jordan and Jeremy started out at a brisk walk, at least while their mom could see them. But once they were out of her sight, they speeded up to a jog, and then a slow lope on a level part of the trail. They needed to cover ground to complete their mission in time. They soon arrived at Chip's house, where Chip and Molly were waiting.

Rocket was saddled, and Chip was holding his camera, cell phone, poncho, first aid kit, official Rider canteen, a huge lunch, and a bag of candy. For lunch, Chip had packed sandwiches, chips, string cheese, crackers, and an apple. Jordan and Jeremy watched while he stuffed his saddlebags full of food.

Jordan exclaimed, "Wow, Chip, did you empty out your kitchen?"

Chip replied, "Not really. I just thought I'd bring a few essentials along. A Rider has to be prepared, you know."

"Prepared for a famine?" Jordan grinned at his best friend.

Jeremy thought about the small lunches he and Jordan had packed and was a little envious. They each just had a sandwich and an apple in the saddlebag tied behind their saddles.

"We had no problem getting permission to go for a ride! Ya' know, being good does pay off," Jordan said as Chip tightened Rocket's cinch.

"I know what you mean. My mom didn't even stop to think about it when I asked her if I could go for a ride with you guys this morning," Chip said. "Say, have you got the money?"

"Of course we do. We brought $60.00. More than enough!" Jordan said. "Let's go!"

"Too bad Molly can't come," Jeremy said as they waited for Chip to mount Rocket.

Chip said, "Yeah, well, her wings have been clipped for the weekend. Mom is trying to teach her a lesson, I guess. Molly was pretty scared when she was lost, though. I bet she'll be lots more careful in the future, and not go wandering off by herself again anytime soon. At least I hope not."

Jordan and Jeremy checked the cinches on their saddles to make sure they were tight. Then Chip swung up into his saddle and they all rode down the driveway. Jeremy looked back at Molly and her dust rag and waved. "Poor Molly," he thought. "And on such a nice day, too."

They rode on at a brisk jog for three miles on the lightly traveled gravel roads. They stopped periodically for a snack from Chip's stash of candy. Soon they arrived at OK Office Supplies. They all dismounted, and Jordan and Chip handed their reins to Jeremy, who was the designated horse-holder. Luckily, the horses were fairly tired, and stood quietly.

"Sure hope we have time to print out the pictures at my house today when we get back," Chip said. "What time do you have to be home?"

"We can be out until 2 or 3 today. So, depending on what your parents are doing, we just might be able to," Jeremy said. "Hey, Chip, by the way, did you remember to write down the model number of your printer so we know what kind of ink to buy?" Jeremy asked.

"Ugh, no. Aren't all ink cartridges the same?"

The two boys stopped walking and looked at each other.

"Great!" Jordan said "Now what do we do? We can't take a chance and buy the wrong kind. Then we'll have to wait until next Saturday to come back."

"Don't worry," Jeremy said as he reached in his pocket. "I wrote down the model number last Wednesday when I was helping Molly with her homework. I have it right here."

Jordan grabbed the crumpled up piece of paper Jeremy had pulled from his pocket, flashed him a smile and a wink and led the way into the store. Since it was the only store they could ride their horses to, they went there as often as they could, when they had money of course, and they knew where everything was, by aisle number.

"Come on," Jordan yelled, almost running, "Aisle 6. Computer supplies."

The boys rushed down the aisle and then came to a standstill. There were so many different kinds of photo paper they didn't know what to buy.

"Get the cheapest," Chip said, "then we'll have more money left over in case we need to buy more stuff we haven't thought of yet."

"Good thinkin' Chip," Jordan said. "Here's 25 sheets for $19.00; here's one that has 40 sheets for $15.00."

"Get that pack. Better to have extra sheets and extra money!" Chip said. "Now, let's go find the ink cartridge we need."

Jordan looked again at the model number Jeremy had written down and read out loud. "KL-59011. OK, OK......got it! Here it is - a three pack of colors. Holy Moly! It's $40.00! So much for extra money."

"We have to have it," Chip said. "I promise I'll get a Grow jar and start saving up money to pay you guys back. But, we have to have this NOW!"

"Relax, Chip. We'll get it." Jordan said as he pulled the package off the shelf.

The boys paid for the paper and ink and bought three cans of Coke. Jordan picked up a comic book for himself. "You can read it next week, after I'm done," he told Chip.

Once outside again, they took their horses back from Jeremy, and handed him a can of Coke. He opened it cautiously. Expecting that Jordan had shaken it up before handing it to him, he was afraid he'd spray Penny with pop. But, Jordan hadn't shaken the can at all, which surprised Jeremy just a little.

They carefully packed the ink and paper in Jordan's saddle bag so they wouldn't get damaged, no matter what. Jordan took a look at Chip's bulging saddlebag and asked, "What else have you got in there, Chip, a telescope or something?"

"Nope, just the essentials," grinned Chip. With time growing short, the boys mounted up and headed for Chip's house. They stopped for a few minutes in a shady spot in a field to eat their lunches and finish the cokes. They each ate an apple, and gave the cores to their horses, then rode back to Chip's house as fast as they could without over-working the horses.

When they reached the house, the boys couldn't believe their luck! Chip's mom and dad were both working outside on the roses. Actually, it appeared that Mrs. Easton was doing the work while Mr. Easton snoozed nearby in a chaise lounge chair, holding the garden hose.

"Great!" Chip said. "We'll have at least an hour to ourselves before they come inside and wonder what we're up to. Let's go!"

They waved to Mr. and Mrs. Easton as they rode to the stable to tie up their horses. They rushed through the whole process, which was something they usually spent a lot of time doing. But, they had evidence to gather.

Molly was anxiously waiting for them at the door. "Come on, I've been watching for you for a half hour. Mom and Dad just went out to work on the roses. They're weeding and pruning so they'll be out there a long time! I have the computer and printer turned on, ready to go!"

Chip ran into his room to grab his camera while Jordan and Jeremy followed Molly into the family room. They went right to work. Jeremy opened up their package of paper, took the other paper out and put their paper in, just as planned. Jordan opened up the color ink cartridge and got it ready to install. Chip was fumbling with his camera making sure he knew how to hook it up to the computer so they could print out the pictures.

"Here, Chip, let me do that," Jordan said. "I've watched my dad do this a thousand times. Put the ink cartridges in. "

Once the camera was installed, and the printer was loaded, Chip started pulling up all the photos they had taken. "Wow! We've got 41 photos! I didn't know we took that many!"

"Well, let's start looking at them one at a time. Let's try to print out at least ten, but only the best ten. That should be enough. Molly, you keep an eye out for your parents. Let us know the second they start heading toward the house," Jeremy said.

"OK. But I want to see the pictures, too."

"Oohh…look at that one! Let's print it," Chip said pointing to a picture of the passenger door of the red sports car.

"Hold on," Jordan said. "Chip, write down the file name, then put a star by it. Once we have at least ten pictures listed with stars by their names, we'll print them all out. Let's not start printing out pictures until we've looked at all of them."

The boys managed to work together very well. Chip would open a picture, they would all look at it, then vote on if it was good enough to print. To be good enough, it had to be clear, and had to be of a different car entering, leaving or sitting in Carson's driveway. When they agreed on a picture, Jeremy wrote down the file name and put a star by it.

After about an hour, they had looked at 24 pictures and ended up with a total of 16 pictures on their print list.

"Let's start printing," Jordan said. As soon as the first picture rolled out of the printer, Chip remarked confidently, "We've got him now for sure. These are gonna be great!"

Jordan agreed after two more pictures came out of the printer. "These are great," he said. "You can really tell the make and model of each car. Just can't make out the license number on some of these. They all seem too dirty to read."

Chip pulled open the drawer of the computer desk and pulled out a magnifying glass. He inspected the photos carefully. "I bet the forensics team can make them out, just like on CSI," he declared.

"Hey, what time is it?" Jordan asked.

"It's 1:30. We better stop," Jeremy said.

"OK. Chip, let me have those pictures. Do you have a school book or something I could put 'em in? I don't want our parents wondering what I'm carrying around."

"Even better! Jeremy left a Math workbook here when he was helping Molly with her homework."

"I don't need it — it's from third grade. Don't know why I still had it anyway," Jeremy said.

"Awesome!" Jordan said. "Go get it so I can put the pictures in it. Jeremy, we better get going. Molly, where are your parents?"

"Still with the roses," Molly said. "Now can I look at the pictures?"

"Sure, but hurry up." Jordan handed Molly the pictures one at a time.

Chip ran back in the family room just as Jeremy was replacing the paper and cartridge in the printer. Jordan stuffed the pictures in the middle of the Math workbook while Jeremy packed up their photo paper and ink cartridge.

"OK! We're ready. And remember everybody, stay on your best behavior next week. Just in case we need to come back after school a couple days next week, NO GETTING GROUNDED!"

Once on their horses, the boys waved goodbye to Chip and Molly, and to their parents, who were still gardening. They rode back home more slowly than they had started. They knew they had to bring their horses back cool, rather than hot and sweaty; their mom had made that very clear.

Once back at their farm, they hosed down both horses with cool water before turning them out into the pasture. Jordan groaned when he saw Banner rolling vigorously in his favorite sandy spot in the paddock. "No wonder he's always so dusty. What a piggy!"

"Maybe Penny won't roll. She's more ladylike anyway," Jeremy said hopefully. "Too late, down she goes!"

Their mom came out to say hello and noticed Jordan taking the math workbook out of his saddle bag.

"What's that?"

"Oh, it's one of Jeremy's math books. He left it at Chip's house when he helped Molly with her homework last week."

Just then, both horses stood up, and were caked with sand from head to hoof. "You'll have some heavy-duty grooming to do tomorrow before you ride," Mrs. Chambers said as she went into the house.

The boys nodded, and followed her. Jeremy was a little green around the gills from all of Chip's candy and snacks he ate. He went up to his room to lie down for a few minutes to let his stomach settle. His mom felt his forehead and said, "No fever, maybe it's something you ate."

Jeremy nodded wanly. Jordan, who had an iron stomach, went back outside to the tree house, and settled in for some quality time with his game boy. After an hour or so, he heard piano music wafting through the window, so he knew Jeremy was feeling better. By the time dinner rolled around, neither boy felt like eating much.

To keep up appearances, Jordan managed to eat a grilled cheese sandwich and bowl of tomato soup, while Jeremy managed only a small bowl of soup. That night, the family played Monopoly together, and then played a game of hearts. Jordan and Jeremy noticed their dad looking longingly at the TV, and he was soon engrossed in watching a ballgame. The boys were tired out, and went willingly to bed early; both boys had visions of cars in Carson's driveway as they drifted off to sleep.

The following Tuesday night, Mrs. Easton called Mrs. Chambers and spoke in a low voice about how changed Chip and Molly seemed to be after the camping mishap. "Do you think it'll last?" She asked her friend.

"I don't know, but it seems to have rubbed off on Jordan and Jeremy. They've been almost like little angels since the moment we got home. Hard to believe!"

"And the way all four of them want to hang around together, I can't believe they're including Molly. It's unbelievable. I was so impressed with Jeremy last week when he came over and helped Molly with her math homework. What a sweet thing to do. And then, this afternoon Chip asked me if Jordan and Jeremy can come over after school more often to help him – and Molly – with their homework. It's fine with me, if it's OK with you."

"Sure! Mrs. Chambers replied. "I'm thrilled and very proud of them. Thanks for putting up with them. Just let me know if they become too much trouble."

At that very moment, the two "angels" were in fact having a very quiet argument out of Mrs. Chambers' earshot. Jordan pounded Jeremy hard on the upper arm, and Jeremy retaliated with a punch of his own. "Sh, or she'll hear us," Jordan whispered.

"Yeah, you're right. We can't get in trouble for at least another week – just in case we have to go back to Chip's to print out more pictures," Jeremy whispered back.

The boys stopped fighting, and walked down the hallway with their arms draped across each other's shoulders, and a somewhat forced smile on their faces.

Mrs. Chambers almost dropped the phone when she saw that. "As a matter of fact, Jordan and Jeremy have never acted this good, even before Christmas!" she told Mrs. Easton. "Maybe we should go camping more often. It seems to be really good for them. They've bonded more."

"Easy for you to say, you didn't have an eight year old missing for three hours," Mrs. Easton replied.

"Yes, that was scary. But, I think it shook our kids up in a good way. I certainly don't ever want another scare like that during the next camping trip, but I sure would like our kids to come back the same way they did this time. I wonder if the upcoming parade and horse show will have a similar effect."

"Oh, that's right," Mrs. Easton exclaimed. "Those events are coming up soon, aren't they? Anyway, just wanted to let you know your boys are welcome to come over any time. They've been a real pleasure."

"That's good to know. Thanks for calling," Mrs. Chambers said as she hung up the phone and began preparing dinner.

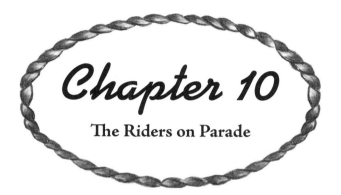

Chapter 10
The Riders on Parade

As the next Frolic Riders meeting night approached, all four kids were eager to attend. This was the meeting when they were going to get the pictures to Amanda. Jordan had them neatly organized in an envelope that he packed in his saddle bag. But, when they arrived at the meeting, Amanda had a bit of a surprise for them. As they settled into their seats, Amanda began the meeting with an announcement.

"As you know, our Spring parade is coming up. But this year, it's not just the usual parade. It's to qualify to ride in the Summer parade next month, that'll be on TV!"

There was an excited buzz as the Riders of all ages started talking at once. Amanda held up her hand for order, and the troop eventually quieted down.

"Not everyone can ride in this parade," she explained. "You have to qualify, which means you need to practice! Tryouts will take place next Saturday, before the regular meeting starts."

After about a minute of mumbling and stirring from the excited, but anxious Riders, Amanda continued. "If you want to qualify, you have to practice to make sure your horse or pony won't get spooked by flags waving and bands playing nearby. Maybe practice with some loud music playing. And wave a flag near your horse until he stays calm. Then mount and wave a flag around. But be careful the first time for sure. We don't want any accidents."

The parents who were nearby and heard this, groaned audibly. They knew they were in for flag duty for the next few days.

"Well," Chip said to Jordan. "So much for giving Amanda the pictures tonight."

"Well, maybe not tonight, but for sure during the tryouts." Jordan said. "I'll find a way somehow to get Amanda's attention long enough to hand her the pictures."

Each day the following week, Jordan and Jeremy practiced with Banner and Penny trying to ride at a walk alongside each other, while taking turns carrying a flag. They played some loud marching music from an old CD player that was in the stable. Their mom supervised the operation for the first few days, until she was sure the horses, and her boys, were steady. Banner did great from the start, due to his horse show experience but it took until Wednesday before Penny settled down.

"I'm sure you'll both be picked to be in the parade," Mrs. Chambers said at dinner that night. After all, Banner and Penny are both beautiful horses. We'll have them shiny clean for next Saturday. And you should clean your tack too."

"Can we put the shiny black stuff on their hooves?" asked Jeremy.

"Sure. And I can braid their manes for you, in a nice French braid with a cute bow." She added.

Jordan sputtered, "Not Banner! He's a boy horse and doesn't want braids and bows. Maybe Penny does."

Jeremy, who normally would have shoved his brother hard or at least snapped back at him, refrained. It was odd, but after the week they spent "pretending" to be great friends, it was becoming more natural for the two boys to get along like good friends.

"Penny is a bright chestnut, and with her white stockings, she looks flashy. Maybe I'll give her a nice braid, but no bow," Mrs. Chambers said.

Jeremy agreed. "And I'll put the shiny stuff on her hooves."

By Friday, both boys were nervous but well prepared for the parade tryouts. The tack was clean, their boots polished, their uniforms were crisp and neat. Jordan had decided to perk up Banner's appearance with four white dressage wraps on his legs, and a fluffy white saddle pad to match. Jeremy had a fluffy white saddle pad for Penny, too.

On Saturday morning, they trailered the horses over to the tryouts and meeting. They first learned that each Elite Rider automatically qualified which meant that a set of two white Arabian horses, a coal black gelding, and Amanda's gorgeous palomino would be leading them in the parade. Two showy pintos belonging to Junior Riders were then quickly selected.

Jeremy and Penny rode alongside several other chestnut horses, with flags waving directly in front and behind them. Penny stayed steady and kept the right pace alongside the other chestnuts about her size. When Jeremy and his mom saw the nods from the Elite Rider judges, they smiled at each other, excited that Penny was chosen to be in the parade.

Jordan nervously awaited his turn with other bay horses. At least Banner wasn't nervous. Rocket, on the other hand, kept shaking his head up and down nervously, and then pawing with his front hooves. He hated waiting. Chip was getting frustrated by Rocket's antics.

"At least he's ambidextrous," Jordan said after Rocket pawed with alternating hooves.

Finally it was Jordan's turn. He and Banner were supposed to walk next to the other bay horses, and stay even with them. It sounded easier than it was, but Jordan and Banner did well and were selected after a short time. The flags hadn't bothered Banner in the least, thanks to their practicing.

Chip and Rocket did not fare quite so well. Rocket shied away from the flags, refused to walk alongside the other horses, and was always either in front or behind. They were not selected to perform in the parade, but Chip was tapped to be in the pooper-scooper detail, which entailed carrying a broom and shovel, and walking behind the horses in the troop. "At least I have new boots that fit," Chip thought to himself as he heard the not so great news. He knew he'd be doing a lot of walking and shoveling.

"Thanks a lot, Rocket," Chip muttered to his trusty steed, noticing that peculiar glint in Rocket's eye again. Chip could have sworn the horse was laughing at him, once again.

Then it was Molly's and Midnight's turn. They were lined up with several other small ponies in pairs, and did very well. Molly was able to control Midnight, while some of the other ponies would occasionally stop to nibble on grass, or just look around. One grey pony in particular was having none of it, and was instead eating grass quite contentedly while her young owner tugged on the reins and drummed with her heels in vain to get her going forward.

Noticing that there were two small black ponies that seemed to handle well, Amanda suggested that those two ponies, one of which was Midnight, would look cute up front, with the riders holding the troop's banner between them. Molly noticed that Mr. Grimmer was rapidly shaking his head no, but apparently Amanda hadn't noticed. Two of the Elite Riders quickly handed the troop's banner to Molly and a small boy named Derek, who was on his black pony named Jet. The two Cadets practiced holding it between them, while riding a few feet apart. They soon had the hang of it.

After all horses and riders were chosen, the troop had a practice run.

Following Molly and Derek, who were proudly holding the Frolic Riders banner, were the color guard. They were mounted on pretty white horses and carrying the U.S. flag and the Michigan state flag. Amanda on her beautiful palomino, and Tyler, a fellow Elite Rider, on his big black gelding, were next, followed by the flashy pintos and some matching grey horses.

Jeremy and Penny rode with the other chestnut horses, with Penny on the outside because she was shorter than the others. Jordan and Banner followed behind with the other bay horses. A couple of flashy appaloosas, followed by a few other hand-picked Junior Riders rode behind them. Last of all came the support crew, including Chip and Tony, another Junior Rider who hadn't been selected to ride. The remaining Cadets and Junior Riders who were not selected to ride or do pooper-scooper detail, marched on foot behind the horses and riders. One of the parents was working with them on their marching.

They spent almost an hour parading around the large riding ring, then down the dirt road. When they returned, the Riders lined up in neat rows to listen to the Elite Riders and their ideas. Amanda said, "It looks good, but it's missing something. There's no flash."

Terrence, one of the other Elite Riders, agreed. "Yeah I know what you mean. The 4-H Club Riding Rascals, are going as clowns. Their horses will be wearing clown ruffles and stuff like that. They'll attract more attention than us for sure."

"What we need is sizzle, but no clowns please! Anyone have any ideas?" Amanda asked.

"Some of the dressage show horses could do a sort of prance when we're in front of the reviewing stand. We have some horses that can do a nice half pass, or a passage, and that might attract attention." Tyler commented.

Before Tyler had even finished talking, Jordan envisioned he and Banner doing the half pass, which was a beautiful traverse trot in which the horse moved diagonally, crossing over both front and back legs gracefully.

Amanda beamed. "Good idea! We can put them right behind the color guard."

That gave Jordan another idea. Surprising even himself, he spoke up loudly, "Banner can do the Spanish Walk. That would get attention."

Several of the Riders piped up "No way!" A few didn't know what the Spanish Walk was, and Amanda explained that it was a high level movement in which the horse strutted at the walk, almost like goose-stepping. It was very beautiful when done well.

Jordan insisted that he could do it, and moved Banner over closer to where his mom was standing. He whispered to her "What was Banner's cue for Spanish Walk? I can't remember."

She quickly whispered directions to him. Jeremy crossed his fingers and waited anxiously as Jordan moved Banner to the front where everyone could see them. Banner took two normal steps, and then realized what Jordan wanted. Banner enthusiastically performed a flawless Spanish Walk all the way across the ring. With his tail held high, and his neck arched gracefully, Banner looked gorgeous. The troop was thrilled and applauded Banner and Jordan.

"OK, Jordan," Amanda said. "You and Banner are in with the Spanish Walk."

Jeremy and Molly beamed and applauded with the rest. Their mom looked so proud. Chip had a sickly grin on his face and couldn't bring himself to applaud his friend and Banner. He had his hands full with Rocket anyway.

With the new parade assignments made, the troop started to pack up and head for home. As Amanda was jotting down notes on her clipboard, Jordan approached her.

Hanging on tightly to the envelope with the pictures in it, Jordan said. "Thanks, Amanda, for letting me and Banner in the parade. We won't let you down. We're way better at the Spanish Walk than I am at vaulting. Amanda, do you remember the pictures we talked about?"

"Pictures?" Amanda asked. "What pictures?"

"Of Mr. Carson's chop shop. You said if we got you pictures of the stolen cars on his property, you would show them to your dad so he could arrest him."

"Oh yeah. OK. Let me have them and I'll give them to my dad."

"Thanks. You won't lose them will you? These weren't easy to get." Jordan said as he handed Amanda the envelope.

"No, I won't lose them and I won't forget," Amanda replied, a bit annoyed, as she clipped the envelope to her clipboard. "I'll let you know what he says at our next parade practice."

Feeling very accomplished, Jordan went to join his mom and Jeremy who were getting Penny and Banner safely in their trailer.

Jordan and Jeremy both were excited on the way home, and talked about practicing hard for the next two weeks before the parade. Several additional practices had been scheduled to make sure the troop would look its best. As soon as they got home and unloaded the horses and gear, both boys climbed into the tree house to talk things over. Jeremy used the rope steps near the tree trunk, while Jordan climbed nimbly up the rope.

When they were both in, Jeremy asked Jordan, "Did you give Amanda the pictures?"

Jordan replied, "Sure. While everybody was packing up. She put them on her clipboard so she wouldn't lose them, but we didn't have much time to talk."

"Great," Jeremy exclaimed. "Now we'll be able to wrap up the Skeleton Creek Caper for sure!"

They left the tree house and went inside. They were hungry and each grabbed an apple from the fruit bowl as they went their separate ways. Jordan went upstairs to play on the computer and Jeremy headed for the piano. Jordan started to say something bratty to Jeremy about practicing the piano but then stopped himself. Like Jeremy, Jordan discovered that pretending to get along with Jeremy had rubbed off on him; teasing him just didn't make much sense any more.

He thought back at how much he couldn't stand it when Jeremy first started getting good at the piano. He had to admit that it was probably because his younger brother immediately out shown him when they first took lessons together. Because Jeremy was younger than him, Jordan expected to be better than him at everything. But when it came to playing the piano, that just wasn't the case. As Jordan listened to Jeremy playing, he felt kind of relieved that it didn't bother him much anymore.

He called down to Jeremy, "I'm glad we both get to be in the parade. Penny looked awesome out there."

Jeremy was so surprised he almost fell off the piano bench. He stopped playing for a second and told his brother thanks.

"Banner did great," he said. "You should have seen Chip's face when Banner did that perfect Spanish Walk. I didn't know you'd been practicing it."

"I didn't practice it. But horses never forget once they're trained to do something. Mom will help me with him these next couple of weeks, so we'll really nail it in the parade," Jordan said.

Jeremy could smell something delicious cooking, and asked his mom when they were having dinner. She told him one hour so Jeremy stayed at the piano. A few minutes later, Jordan walked in the kitchen, attracted by the aroma of chicken baking in the oven. He set the table without his usual fuss, which put his mother in an even better mood. Soon, Jeremy and their dad joined Jordan and their mom.

While the three "men of the house" sat at the table anxiously awaiting dinner, Jordan told his dad about their success at the parade tryouts. Soon dinner was served. The three Chambers men looked eagerly at one of their favorite meals, roast chicken, mashed potatoes, green beans, biscuits and honey, and tossed salad.

"I thought we'd have a feast tonight to celebrate the parade results," Mrs. Chambers said as she sat at the table.

The boys were starving, and wolfed down a couple of pieces of chicken each, a mountain of mashed potatoes, a generous helping of beans, several biscuits each, and a little bit of salad. Their mom was pleased to see such good appetites, but was dismayed that there was so little left over for dinner the next day. She managed to keep enough potatoes to make potato pancakes with sour cream or apple sauce for the next day's dinner.

As she and Mr. Chambers cleared the table, she commented, "When they become teenagers, I'll feel like I'm feeding an army, at this rate. I don't see how they stay so slim."

"Exercise," their dad replied. "They stay active out here. No sitting around watching TV or a computer screen all the time. My long commute to work is worth it so they can grow up out here, and not in the city."

"Yes, but I do wish your drive wasn't quite so long," Mrs. Chambers added. "I'm so lucky I can work from home most of the time."

Jordan and Jeremy overheard the conversation and joined in.

"I'd never give up Banner, and Jeremy would never give up Penny. There's nowhere I'd rather live," declared Jordan.

"Me too," agreed Jeremy.

For the next two weeks, the boys settled into a routine of school, homework and parade practices. There were three formal troop practices before the parade. At each one, Jordan desperately tried to get Amanda's attention to find out what her dad had said or done with the pictures. But, she didn't have a minute to herself. Jordan finally gave up, figuring he'd have a chance after the parade was over, which seemed like forever to Jordan and Jeremy. They could hardly contain their excitement at competing to be on television in the Summer parade.

Parade day finally arrived. It was a bright and clear Saturday. Jordan and Jeremy were so excited they could hardly choke down their Cheerios that morning. Their mom made toast with peanut butter, which both boys loved, and sliced up some red ripe strawberries for their cereal. Their dad stumbled into the kitchen, reaching out almost blindly for his mug of coffee.

"Did we have to get up this early? The parade doesn't start till noon," he said.

Jordan piped up, "Oh, we have to be there by 10:30 to get ready for formation at 11a.m. sharp. We still have to feed and water everyone, and groom Penny and Banner. We're all packed though. It'll take an hour to get there too."

Jeremy piped up, "We have to be there early so Mom can French braid their manes."

Their dad groaned, "They'll look like sissies if she puts cute little bows in their manes, like when she showed Banner."

Their mom harrumphed and said firmly, "No bows, but the braids will look nice and professional. It is a judged parade, you know."

Mr. Chambers sighed and sipped his steaming coffee, clutching his big mug like a lifeline. He liked to sleep in on the weekends. No luck today.

After finishing a quick breakfast, the boys rushed out to the barn to feed all of the animals, then groom Banner and Penny carefully. They each had a bath the night before, so they were already pretty clean. The boys returned to the house to shower, change clothes, comb their hair and brush their teeth.

First they loaded both of the horses, with their parent's supervision. Their dad finally seemed more alert. When he saw the load of gear they were stowing in the back of the SUV, and the horse tack loaded into the trailer compartment, his mouth dropped open. "It's just one parade, right? We're not staying overnight, right?"

"Yes, dear. Please bring the cooler with our lunch and snacks, and put it in the back with the rest of the boys' things," Mrs. Chambers asked.

That was when Mr. Chambers made his huge mistake. He nonchalantly lifted the heavy cooler, felt something pull in his back, dropped the cooler on his foot, and moaned in pain. "Ow! Why didn't you tell me it was that heavy? I think I put my back out," he complained.

"I thought you'd get the boys to help you. Are you ok?" Mrs. Chambers asked, very concerned.

Not wanting to appear weak in front of his sons, he nodded feebly, then hobbled over to the passenger's seat, and crawled into the SUV gratefully. He didn't usually drive the SUV when hauling horses. Jordan and Jeremy's eyes widened to see their dad clutching his back and hobbling like that.

"Oh, he'll be fine, boys, not to worry," their mom reassured them. "Help me with this cooler, please."

The three of them soon managed to get the heavy cooler into the back of the vehicle. Their mom ran through a list of things they needed and Jordan carefully checked them off, with Jeremy close by his elbow. Once everything was onboard, off they drove to the parade ground.

When they arrived at the staging area, it was complete chaos. Horses were whinnying, and stamping their hooves impatiently. Children were running around excitedly. The Chambers found a space to park, and thankfully it was far away from the two high school marching bands.

"I don't know where all our rigs are going to park. No one will want to be next to those bands. Lucky thing we got here early," their mom commented.

Soon they unloaded the horses and gave them one final polish before they were tacked up and ready to go. Their mom braided each mane neatly as promised, then glittered them. With their hooves polished as a finishing touch, Banner and Penny seemed alert and eager. Even when the trumpets blared and the cymbals crashed, neither horse was frightened.

The boys were spiffy-looking, dressed in their full dress uniforms, complete with black helmets and shiny black boots. Each wore a colorful red sash, proudly displaying his hard-earned merit badges. Jordan noticed that he had a couple more than Jeremy, but decided not to point that out.

Finally, Molly, Chip, and Midnight arrived. Since they were so late, they had to park next to a high school band, which was practicing at an ear-splitting level. Chip, in his dress uniform, was bending over Midnight, applying the shiny black hoof polish. Just then, a trombone section blasted a loud note, not quite in tune, either, according to Jeremy. Midnight did not take kindly to all the commotion, and jerked his feet nervously, just as Chip was applying the black polish. Inky black polish sprayed all over Chip's uniform shirt, staining it badly.

"Oh Chip," his mom sighed, after Midnight settled down.

Chip looked down at his stained uniform and asked desperately, "You can fix it, can't you, Mom?"

"Not right now, Chip. I'll take it to the cleaners on Monday and see what they can do. Do your best to wipe it up. We've got to get to the staging area, or we'll be late."

Chip's mouth tightened in frustration. Molly consoled him, "Midnight says he's sorry, Chip."

Chip snarled something that was luckily unintelligible. Just then Jordan and Jeremy walked up with Banner and Penny. The boys looked splendid in their pristine uniforms with well-groomed horses. The boys' eyes widened when they saw Chip's uniform, but they wisely said nothing after noticing Chip's scowl. They all walked together toward the rest of the troop, leading the three steeds. They couldn't walk very fast, because their dad was hunched over, hobbling painfully alongside his sons.

Once they made it to their troop's staging area, Jordan, Jeremy, and Molly mounted up. Their moms wiped off their boots, straightened their ties, and wished them good luck. Chip was still scowling. To take his mind off his sorry state, Jordan asked him where his dad was.

"He didn't get home until early this morning. He had to get a couple hours of sleep, but he promised to come later in the day to see us in the parade."

Molly chimed in, "Daddy wouldn't miss it! He said so."

They soon met up with the rest of the troop. Mr. Grimmer, holding a large megaphone, and sharply dressed in his uniform, directed them to line up as they had practiced. Molly and Midnight rode up next to Derek and Jet. Mrs. Easton was given the troop banner to hold for safekeeping. She smiled at her daughter, who looked adorable in her Cadet uniform, sitting proudly on her darling black pony.

Mr. Grimmer directed Jordan and Banner right behind the color guard, and Jeremy and Penny slipped easily into line with the other pretty chestnut horses. Mr. Grimmer saw Chip standing around glumly, and he directed him to get the broom and shovel to clean up any mishaps he could find now. Then he was to take his place behind the troop horses, and in front of the Junior Riders and Cadets who were marching on foot.

Mr. Grimmer looked more carefully at Chip and said, "Your uniform is a disgrace, Chip. What happened?"

"Sorry, Mr. Grimmer. I had an accident with the hoof polish a few minutes ago." Chip apologized.

He breathed a sigh of relief as Mr. Grimmer's attention was drawn to a problem with the pintos, who were acting up. Then Chip's pooper-scooper partner Tony walked over, wheeling a large decorated wheelbarrow, and looking none too happy about it. Chip could understand Tony's dismay at having to push a smelly wheelbarrow for the whole parade route. Chip got busy cleaning up several recent piles of droppings, but realized he had the better job than Tony. At least Tony's uniform was clean, Chip thought enviously.

Meanwhile, Jordan and Jeremy's excitement turned to nervousness once they were all lined up and ready to go. They could see loads of people lining the street ahead. Jordan, in particular, had a bad case of butterflies. His mom patted Banner and spoke a few words privately to him. Jordan realized how steady Banner was, and sat up a little straighter in his saddle. He concentrated on keeping his heels down, and elbows in. He knew that Banner would do them proud, and then, he wasn't nervous anymore. Mr. Chambers was standing, a bit crookedly, near Jeremy and Penny, who both seemed fine. Jordan turned a little in the saddle and grinned back at his brother. Jeremy smiled back, a little nervously.

Just when the troop was set to go, in came the clowns from the Riding Rascals 4-H group. They were all in colorful clown outfits. Their head rider, who often competed in horse shows against Amanda, sneered at her and said, "Nice turnout. Too bad you're going to lose. You've got no pizzazz!"

Amanda replied in a dignified manner, "We'll see about that."

She and Tyler signaled the troop to move out.

The troop performed beautifully, much to the relief of the young riders and their parents. Molly and Derek led the way, with Mr. Grimmer riding off on one side, directing their pace. He was pleasantly surprised to see how well Molly and Midnight were doing with the troop's banner. The crowd cheered to see the two little Cadets astride the cute ponies.

Amanda and Tyler led the troop, prancing along the parade route. The color guard followed with their pretty white horses. Next came Banner and Jordan, who put on a show. Banner pranced along proudly in a beautiful passage movement. Every few minutes, Jordan slowed him down and cued him for the Spanish Walk. Banner came through like a champ. He strutted, with his front legs reaching out impossibly far in a perfect Spanish Walk. The crowd gasped, and then cheered to see the beauty of the steps.

The other horses kept in good order behind him, with some flashy steps by a few of the best trained horses. The crowd showed much appreciation, with plenty of applause. A few people chuckled when they saw Tony and Chip, who had decided to make the best of their assignment. They kept their heads held high, and went about their cleanup duty efficiently and with good humor, occasionally waving at people in the crowd.

As the troop passed the judge's stand, they made an extra effort to keep their lines straight and to sit tall in the saddle. Banner, whose coat glistened with sweat from the effort he was making, had perfect form as he passed in front of the judges. Jordan overheard one of the judges make a comment about the gorgeous bay horse. From the corner of his eye, Jordan saw the judges conferring. He smiled, and was so proud of his good horse. Jeremy was doing fine with Penny. All he had to do was keep her in line with the other chestnuts in his row, and Penny seemed to understand what he wanted.

At the end of the parade route, all of the Riders dismounted and led their horses back to the staging area to await the results of the judging. Jordan and Jeremy were happy to see their mom, who had hustled over quickly, and was going over both horses with a trained eye. After she was sure they were ok, with a final pat for each, she handed each son an ice cold can of pop. That was a nice treat to be sure, because the Chambers boys weren't often allowed to drink soda pop. Jeremy finally saw his dad, who had by that time hobbled over to them. Molly and Chip were pleased to see both of their parents; it seems their dad had made it in time to see them march in the parade.

They all anxiously awaited the results. Jordan said he didn't care if they didn't win, just as long as they beat the clowns. Jeremy, Chip, and Molly quickly agreed.

After the horses and Midnight were cooled down, they put them into the horse trailers, and then put away their tack. Both families gathered near the Chambers' tailgate, to enjoy a wonderful picnic lunch together. Their dad's back spasms were starting to subside. Jordan and Jeremy were amazed at the amount of food he was putting away. He claimed he needed the extra nourishment for recovery, but Jordan figured that the delicious cold fried chicken, deviled eggs, veggies with dip, cookies, and brownies that Chip's mom made, along with ice cold slices of watermelon were just too good to pass up. The boys kept up pretty well with their dad, but they made Chip stand downwind to eat, because he smelled a little ripe.

They had just finished eating when Mr. Grimmer came briskly over to the staging area where the whole troop was gathered. He was positively beaming, so the troop figured it was good news. He no sooner announced, "We won!" then bedlam broke out. It was lucky the horses had been put away already, because the cheering and whooping would have upset some of them for sure. Mr. Grimmer told them they were chosen to ride in the televised Summer parade next month.

After he was able to calm them down, he selected the Elite Riders, along with Molly, Derek, and Jordan to accept the trophy at the ceremony. He had Molly and Derek carry the troop banner, and the others marched behind as they went over to the reviewing stand where the judges stood. Jeremy looked quickly at his mom, and thought he saw her wipe away a tear or two.

Jeremy said firmly, "I knew Banner and Jordan could do it." His parents beamed with pride for their horses and sons.

After the parade award ceremony, in which the 4-H Riding Rascal clowns didn't even place, Mr. Grimmer gathered the Frolic Riders together to hand out well-earned badges. Each of them received a special parade badge, impressively outlined in gold braid. Jordan smiled happily as he accepted his badge. Jeremy looked at his badge proudly, and could hardly wait for his mom to sew it onto his sash when they got home. Molly was thrilled to be one of the two Cadets to earn the golden badge, while the marchers all got plain-looking participation badges.

Then Mr. Grimmer turned toward Chip and Tony and surprised them by presenting each with the golden badge for doing an excellent job on a difficult task. Chip grinned and thanked Mr. Grimmer. He knew that it was his good attitude that earned him the award. Molly was thrilled for Chip, and Jordan and Jeremy pounded him on the back in congratulations. It was a wonderful day for all of the children.

Chapter 11

Back on the Caper

On the morning after the parade, the Chambers family went to church then enjoyed a delicious Sunday dinner. After they were stuffed full of food, Jordan and Jeremy headed toward their tree house to relax and wait for Chip and Molly to arrive. Jordan climbed smoothly up the rope clutching a small notebook in his teeth, wearing binoculars around his neck, with his pockets packed with cards and a pocket knife.

Jeremy climbed carefully up the ladder, carrying both official Frolic Riders canteens around his neck. The boys settled in, and played a few games of Crazy 8's, in between spying outside with the binoculars, watching for Chip and Molly. Suddenly, a small grinning girl was poking her head through the trap door. Jeremy smiled in greeting and said "Hi," to Molly and Chip. Jordan wondered how they managed to sneak up without being noticed.

Molly and Chip looked at each other and grinned again. "We've been practicing our spy techniques," Chip reported to his two friends.

Molly chimed in, "We need to get to work on the Skeleton Creek caper, now that the parade is over. So, let's get back on track and catch some crooks!"

With that said, the four friends put their heads together once again. So far, all they had done was to give Amanda assorted pictures of cars on Carson's property. They also had pictures of a flat bed trailer hauling wrecks out of the yard, and Molly and Jeremy's scrapbook with news clippings of stolen cars and notes about makes and colors of various cars that they thought looked suspicious. And they had the license plate. But no proof of a crime yet.

Chief Morgan didn't seem to be taking any action yet on the photos Amanda said she had given to him. After about an hour of thinking and talking, the four detectives agreed to spend every day of the following week working on the case.

The next day was Memorial Day, which meant a day off school. It also meant that the school year was just about over, and even though Jordan got a wave of excitement by realizing that, he suddenly felt weary as he thought back on all the homework, tests and studying he had done. He sat up and looked out his window. It was going to be a beautiful day. And since the first parade was over, the school year was almost over, and there were four whole weeks before the Summer parade that was to be on TV, Jordan felt he and Jeremy had earned a vacation day. He went into Jeremy's room and just as they were making plans for how they were going to spend the day with Chip and Molly, they found out their mom already had plans for them, that didn't include Chip and Molly.

"Until your rooms are clean, you're not going anywhere. They look like pigsties," Mrs. Chambers said. Both boys sat glumly on Jeremy's unmade bed; they had to admit their bedrooms were a little cluttered.

"Now, get busy!" Mrs. Chambers said walking out of Jeremy's room.

It was a waste of a morning, as far as the boys were concerned. It was noon before the rooms finally passed inspection. Then, after they ate lunch, just as they were about to bolt out the back door to freedom, their mom found a couple other household chores for them to do. She finally turned them loose at one p.m., and the boys immediately saddled up, and rode over to the Eastons.

"What took you so long?" asked Chip.

"We got stuck cleaning our rooms, because Nimrod here left his door open so our mom could see the mess," Jordan complained.

"Nice move, Jeremy," commented Chip.

Molly said, "I bet Jordan's room was just as bad."

"It was worse," said Jeremy. Jordan took the opportunity to pound his brother on the arm, but not nearly as hard as he used to, Jeremy noticed.

"Quit bickering and let's get to work," said Molly impatiently. "I've got an idea. Let's go over to Carson's and spy through the fence again. Just to see what's going on."

"I've been practicing standing up on Banner, so I should be able to see more now than last time," Jordan added. He was anxious to show off his hard-won vaulting skills.

Jeremy had been idly practicing with his lariat, roping a fence post, bucket, and then a rose bush while they had been talking. He managed to knock most of the red roses off the bush too. Molly quickly picked up the rose petals and threw them in the trash so her mom wouldn't see them.

"Jeremy, do you mind?" She complained.

"Sorry," Jeremy said sheepishly. "I was on a roll." He coiled up the lariat and hung it on the saddle, just like Cowboy Bill had taught them at the first fall meeting.

Chip told his mom where they were headed to ride. She was out in the front yard, lovingly attending to the many flowers in bloom. She knew Chip and Jordan would look out for Jeremy and Molly and allowed them to go. She made sure Chip had his cell phone with him in case of an emergency. Chip patted his small saddle pouch that held both his cell phone and camera.

They rode peacefully across the road to the edge of the pasture. Molly looked back and waved cheerily to their mom, and was pleased to see she was heading to their backyard. She wondered how her mom would feel when she saw the rosebush, but quickly put the thought out of her mind.

"Ok, boys. We can speed up now," Molly informed the others.

They speeded up to a jog, then a canter, and were soon at the back of the field. With no one to see them, they cantered along the back of the field to the fence line. Shushing each other, they rode as quietly as possible until they finally found the small peephole near the top of the fence. Jordan maneuvered Banner next to the fence, told him to "Whoa!", and stood right up confidently on his back! Jordan was easily able to see into Carson's yard.

"What do you see?" whispered Chip.

"I see a blue Camaro, a silver car that's been stripped, and a black SUV. No one seems to be around so I can take more pictures," Jordan whispered.

Chip had shown him how to use the camera. He handed it to Jordan who snapped off several photos while standing tall on Banner, peering over the fence. Banner stood like a rock. As soon as Jordan settled back into the saddle, Banner stamped his hooves and shook his head, trying to fend off flies and mosquitoes. He had been careful not to jar his young rider while he was standing atop the saddle.

"Hey, isn't it weird that there used to be a red Camaro and now there's a blue one?" Molly asked.

"Maybe the red one was stolen, and they painted it blue to disguise it!" Chip whispered.

"Or, maybe there are two Camaros, one red and one blue," Jeremy whispered back. "I sure wish the police would raid this place. What's taking so long?"

"They just don't believe us," Jordan whispered. "I'm going to ask Amanda what her dad said about the pictures and the license plate. We should have heard something by now."

Their work done, temporarily at least, the children rode back the same way they came. Slapping at annoying mosquitoes and biting flies, they decided to wear bug spray next time.

"And we need to put some more on the horses, too," said Jeremy, who was using the end of his lariat to flick flies off Penny. She seemed to appreciate it.

All four kids made it back to their homes in time for evening chores, and a hearty supper. Chip and Molly spent time with Chip's camera, looking at the pictures Jordan had taken and reviewing Molly and Jeremy's notes. The only Camaro they had recorded recently was bright red. "It didn't look like it needed a paint job, either," Chip commented.

"So they're stealing cars, bringing them out here, repainting them, then selling them!" Molly exclaimed.

"And sometimes they are stripping them to sell the parts, then junking the frame," Chip said. "I hope Jordan talks to Amanda at vaulting practice this week."

A call to come to dinner interrupted the two young investigators. Chip and Molly went downstairs to join their mom for a dinner of macaroni and cheese, one of their favorites, and a side of broccoli, which was not. Their dad was on the road, even though it was a holiday.

Meanwhile, after Jordan and Jeremy had eaten their dinner and finished the barn chores, Jordan and his dad watched a baseball game while Jeremy and his mom spent the rest of the evening reading. Before they knew it, it was time for bed.

Chapter 12

Summer Vacation
Finally Begins

One bright, sunny day in mid June, Jordan and Jeremy slept in, not needing to get up for school. It was the first day of summer vacation! Their mom soon called them to do chores in the barn. Once their pets had eaten, the stalls had been cleaned, and water buckets filled, the boys came in for breakfast.

Since their mom was outside tending the flowers, the boys ate their cereal in front of the TV. During commercials, they made plans to spend the day outside, riding Banner and Penny, of course, to visit Chip and Molly, and then spend some time in the tree house. Just then, their mom came back inside. She sighed when she saw them eating breakfast in front of the TV.

"Well, boys, it's the first day of summer vacation! Let's get it started on the right foot. We're going to clean the basement!"

Jordan and Jeremy groaned, almost in chorus. They hated it when their mom had big cleaning projects that involved them.

She continued brightly, "Time's a wasting! Let's get busy."

With as much grumbling as they could get away with, Jordan and Jeremy reluctantly trooped downstairs. Their mom loaded them up with mops and bucket, rags, spray cleaner, trash bags, and a broom. While the boys glumly cleaned, Mrs. Chambers started on the laundry on the other side of the basement.

The mops were handy dueling weapons and the boys had a little fun instead of cleaning. Their mom finally had to separate the dueling boys, and have them clean in opposite parts of the basement. They actually used their mops on the floor for a few minutes and noticed that the floor sure did shine in the spots where they mopped.

Fortunately, the phone rang, and when their mom went to answer it, both boys took a break. They had found some of their old toys that their mom planned to donate to charity, and played with them until they heard her start back down the stairs. Just as her feet hit the first step, they quickly grabbed their mops and swished them vigorously on the grimy parts of the floor.

"We've been invited on a trail ride this afternoon by Chip's mom. I told her we would go when the basement is clean," she told the boys.

The boys promptly went into high gear, and finished cleaning the basement in record time. They raced upstairs to change clothes. After Mrs. Chambers busily packed a picnic lunch, they loaded the horses and gear in the trailer, and soon arrived at a local park. This park was very popular among the horsey set, because it had nice trails to explore, but also a shallow river where the horses could wade across. The Chambers parked next to the Eastons. The children rode bareback down to the river. All of them, kids and horses, were eager to take a quick dip on a warm day.

Banner, Penny, and Midnight navigated their way carefully down the rather steep bank, while Rocket and Chip charged ahead quickly. Chip forgot to lean back, and fell over Rocket's head right into the river. Unhurt, but soaking wet, he climbed out of the river and slipped on the bank when he tried to climb up. Chip made it up the bank on his third attempt, and went to retrieve Rocket, who had taken the opportunity to do a little grazing on the grass. He sidled just out of Chip's reach.

"Darn you, Rocket," Chip fumed as he squished after his horse. Jordan kindly rode out of the river and caught Rocket, grabbing his reins before he could move off again.

"Here you go, Chip. Wanna' try again? You gotta' lean way back so you don't fall in the river," Jordan counseled his friend.

"Maybe later. I've got to empty out my boots first." Chip's boots were filled with muddy river water.

He whispered fiercely to Rocket, who had that gleam in his eye. "Why can't you be like Banner?"

When Chip arrived back at the trailers, his mom just sighed when she saw her muddy son. "I took a header into the river," Chip told her, unnecessarily.

"You're not getting into the truck like that. We've got cloth seats. Take those filthy jeans and shirt off, and wrap yourself in this saddle blanket."

She handed him a small pony-sized blanket. Behind the trailer, Chip stripped to his underwear, and quickly wrapped the blanket around his middle. The blanket was so small that it left most of his skin completely exposed to bugs and mosquitoes, which were thick that day.

Scratching hideously, Chip joined his friends for lunch. Jordan chuckled when he saw his friend wrapped in the pink blanket, while Jeremy tried to hide his grin.

Molly piped up, "Hey, who said you could use my saddle blanket?"

"Mom did," Chip said as he glared at her. If looks could kill, Molly would have been dead meat right then.

Just when Chip thought his embarrassment was complete, in rode several of the Elite Riders from their troop, including Amanda and Tyler. Chip turned beet red. Jordan and Jeremy loyally got in front of Chip to shield him somewhat from view.

Amanda called out, "Hi everybody." She caught a glimpse of Chip cowering behind Jordan and Jeremy and said, "Hey, Chip, I sure hope you've got bug spray on, because these skeeters are fierce today."

Jordan chimed in, "Yeah, and the deerflies are even worse."

Amanda rode close to the boys and said in a low tone, "My dad did run that plate finally. He said it came back with No Computer Record Found. So he doesn't think he needs to investigate any further. Sorry, guys. Chip, you've got a big bug on your arm." Amanda said as she rode away with Tyler.

"Tell me about it," muttered Chip, slapping at his arm.

"Well, I guess we're on our own," Jeremy said.

"Yep!" Jordan said. "So much for Amanda's help. Geez, all the pain and suffering I went through being on the vaulting team, it was all for nothing." Jordan moaned as he led the others back to their picnic area.

"Not exactly," Jeremy said, "look how well you can stand on Banner and the other cool things you can do now. Let's just keep spying on Carson and taking pictures. Somehow, some way, it will mean something."

"I suppose", Jordan said. But he wasn't really convinced.

The four of them went back to their trailers in silence. When Mrs. Easton noticed the welts springing up on Chip's back, she said they'd best be heading home. While it was an eventful start to their summer vacation, Chip hoped the rest of the summer would be a little less eventful for him.

Chapter 13
Case Closed

Later that same week, after finishing their morning chores and eating breakfast, Chip and Molly were sitting in their family room, watching cartoons. They had already battled over what to watch, and Molly was sulking in the lazy boy chair, while Chip lounged on the couch.

Their mom had left them alone while she went grocery shopping in peace. She found she spent less and moved quicker when the kids weren't with her. She also thought Chip might be coming down with a cold, and didn't want him spreading germs through the store. Their dad had a rare day off work, and was at the hardware store buying barn paint.

Suddenly, Jake let out a bark, and Molly and Chip looked at up at each other.

"Must be something going on at Carson's," Chip said as he jumped off the couch to grab his camera.

"But, nothing ever happens over there in the morning, this is strange," Molly said as she grabbed the binoculars from a bookshelf.

They both tore out their back door, and crept behind some of their mom's prized butterfly bushes. Chip poked his head and shoulders through the leaves and snapped several photos of a black Corvette being driven through the gate. Mr. Carson looked up and down the road before he swung the gate closed. Chip and Molly noticed the license plate was covered with mud, but the rest of the car was pretty clean.

"The dirt on that license plate is to cover up the license number," whispered Chip.

"Let's call Jordan and Jeremy, and see if they can come over," suggested Molly. They crept back into the house, in case Mr. Carson was watching, and called the Chambers brothers. Jordan and Jeremy entered into a frenzied negotiation with their mom. They promised that if she would let them rush over to Chip and Molly's, they would do a long list of chores when they got back home. With permission granted, the boys made record time in saddling Penny and Banner.

Banner, in particular, seemed dismayed at having his mid-morning nap disturbed, but soon rose to the challenge. The boys started out at a jog until they figured they were out of sight of their mom, and then swung into a ground-covering lope. They made great time, and were soon greeting Molly and Chip at their barn. Rocket and Midnight were saddled and ready to go. The children were armed with the camera, cell phones, and binoculars.

They rode swiftly across the road, and loped all the way to the back of the field, crossing the creek with no problem. Moving as quietly as three horses and a pony possibly could, they rode to their usual peep hole. Jordan stood up on Banner, looked through the hole, and whispered that he could see the black Corvette and the blue Camaro in the yard in front of the pole barn.

Mr. Carson was talking to the driver, who was one of the rough-looking men that he had seen in one of Chip's photos. Jordan signaled to Chip for the camera, who silently handed it to him. Jordan stood tall on Banner's back, and looked over the top of the fence, when he was sure Mr. Carson

The Skeleton Creek Caper

was looking the other way. He was snapping a photo when Chip let out a mighty sneeze. Startled, Mr. Carson and the other man looked right at Jordan's head and at the camera, and started screaming at them.

Jordan dropped down into the saddle, whirled Banner around, and exclaimed, "Let's get out of here!"

Chip and Rocket didn't need to be told twice. With the bit in his teeth, Rocket headed for home so fast that Chip could only cling to his mane and pray that he'd make it back in one piece. Jordan and Banner were galloping smoothly behind him. Penny and Jeremy were right behind him.

Mr. Carson burst out of a side gate in the fence, very close to where Jordan had been standing. He was too late to catch the three boys who raced past him, but Molly on little Midnight didn't stand a chance. Mr. Carson grabbed the reins and jerked Midnight to a stop and tied him to the gate post inside his property. He was yelling as he pulled Molly right off Midnight and dragged her, kicking and screaming, toward the pole barn.

Jeremy heard her scream. He and Penny whirled around quickly and raced toward the open gate and the frightened Molly. Jeremy could see that Mr. Carson was dragging Molly toward the pole barn and he knew what he had to do. With Penny racing along at top speed directly toward Mr. Carson, Jeremy shook out a loop with his lariat. He gave it a swing, and cleanly lassoed Mr. Carson, who was so surprised, he dropped his hold on Molly.

Penny stopped, then backed quickly, pinning Mr. Carson's arms, and jerking him off his feet. Molly ran away from Mr. Carson toward Jeremy and Penny just as fast as her legs would carry her.

Jordan and Banner, meanwhile, had also turned around to help. At a full gallop, Jordan leaned out of the saddle to pick up Molly while she was still running. She scrambled up and situated herself behind his saddle. She held onto Jordan for dear life. Then, Banner with Molly and Jordan aboard, and Penny and Jeremy ran towards Molly's house.

Chip had made it back home safely, and called 911 to report the attempted kidnapping, and the stolen black Corvette and blue Camaro. Then, he called his mother who was still at the grocery store. While racing out of the grocery store, Mrs. Easton called Mr. Easton, at the hardware store. "I'll be there in fifteen minutes," he said.

Jordan, Molly, and Jeremy soon arrived, much to Chip's relief. Jordan called his mom, who nearly became hysterical when she heard that Mr. Carson grabbed Molly right off her pony.

"Stay right there. I'm coming now to get you!" She said as she jumped into their car and sped over.

While driving, she called Mr. Chambers at work, who promised he was on his way. She arrived just as the police pulled up. Mrs. Chambers got out of her car, and hugged both her sons as all three looked up to greet Chief Morgan and another officer.

"When the call came in to Dispatch, and I heard the name and address and I figured I'd better come," Police Chief Morgan told them. Once he saw they were unhurt, he asked, "Now, what exactly is going on here?"

The four children were so excited they all started talking at the same time. The Chief tried to calm them down, and finally pointed at Jordan, whom he remembered from Amanda's vaulting team and the parade. Jordan explained what had happened, and handed the camera to him, so he could see the cars for himself.

Chief Morgan said, "It does seem fishy that Carson was so upset by you kids taking pictures, especially if he wasn't doing anything wrong. And grabbing Molly like that is a crime in itself." He said while viewing the pictures on the camera.

"Let's check it out," he said to the other officer.

"But, what about Midnight?" Molly asked. "How can I get Midnight?"

"I'll get him," Chip said. "If that's OK with you, Chief Morgan."

"Sure, come with us." The two police officers got in the front seat and Chip got in the back seat of the police car. He felt very important until he realized that he was sitting where all the criminals sit when they're being taken to jail. "It's a short ride," Chip muttered to himself.

They arrived on Carson's property and drove right into the yard. For some reason, the front gate hadn't been locked yet. Chief Morgan called for a back up unit.

Chip retrieved Midnight, who was casually munching grass, and the two walked back to his house. Mrs. Easton was racing down the gravel road. When she whipped into the driveway, gravel flew everywhere. She bolted out of the car without shutting the door and ran toward Molly and Chip. She hugged them tightly. Chip squirmed away and Molly said she could hardly breathe, so Mrs. Easton let her go.

After the kids tied Penny, Banner, Rocket and Midnight securely in the barn, they all went into the house. They gathered in the living room and watched out the big window to see what would happen next at Carson's.

"Thank you for getting here so quickly," Mrs. Easton said to Mrs. Chambers. "I was out of my mind with worry driving home."

"Don't mention it," Mrs. Chambers said. "Actually, the boys handled things very well, especially Chip. The police got here a few seconds before I did."

After another minute of staring out the window in silence, they saw Carson and the driver being led out in handcuffs, and put into the second squad car, which drove away. Chief Morgan drove back to the Easton's to talk to the kids and their parents.

By this time, both fathers had arrived too. The parents listened in amazement as the Chief explained that it looked like it was indeed a chop shop operation, and Carson was the ringleader. Apparently, Carson's driver told everything in hopes of getting a lighter sentence. There was plenty of evidence on the property including two stolen cars in the yard, and a couple others in the pole barn.

"You kids did a great job, but you really should leave the detective work to us. You could have been really hurt," Chief Morgan said.

Chip started to speak. He was going to mention the letter they had sent with the license plate number and the pictures they had given to Amanda. Then he decided to just be quiet. He realized that unless it's a 9-1-1 call, kids need an adult with them when they make a crime report.

Mr. Easton was holding Molly in his arms as if he never wanted to let her go. He grabbed Chip and hugged him close, too.

"We should have listened to you before. And we will from now on," Mr. Easton said. "How did you save Molly when Carson grabbed her, Chip?"

"Well, you see," Chip stammered a little, his face turning red.

Molly chimed in quickly, "It was Jeremy! He lassoed Mr. Carson with his rope, and Penny backed up so fast, he fell down with his arms pinned by the rope. Jeremy and Penny saved me first, and then Banner and Jordan picked me up!"

Amazed, everyone turned and looked at Jeremy. Jeremy stood a little taller. He grinned and said, "We did what we had to do. We couldn't let him take Molly!"

Then he added, "You should have seen Jordan and Banner, picking her up like that. At a dead run! They were awesome!"

Jordan blushed with the praise. "Chip and Rocket made it back fast, and they called the police," he reported.

The parents were thankful and proud of each one of them.

Mrs. Chambers spoke for all of the parents when she said, "We're very proud of you for your hard work in solving this crime, but from here on out, please leave the police work to the police, okay?"

All four children nodded in complete agreement. Their detective days were over. Or were they? Summer vacation was just starting, after all.

Discussion Questions

One way to get the most out of this book is if your parents also read it. Then, ask each other these questions and discuss your answers. You may find out something new about your parents when they were young, and they might learn a little more about you, too!

1. Which character in the book would you want as your best friend, and why?

2. Do you have a friend who reminds you of someone in the book? Who is it? Why does he or she remind you of that character?

3. Which horse would you most want to own and why?

4. How do the children demonstrate important values of friendship and loyalty? What other values do they exhibit?

5. Do you think Banner is a magical horse?

6. What did Molly do right when she got lost?

Activity

Do you remember the Give-Grow-Get jars in this story? You can make and use your own jars as a way to handle your money wisely. Here's what you do:

Find three jars or canisters. Decorate the "Give Jar" with a picture of a charity, such as your church, or some other worthy cause. Decorate the second jar, the "Grow Jar" with a picture of something you want to save up to buy. Decorate the "Get Jar" anyway you like, because it is the jar for your spending money. When you receive your allowance, split it equally among the three jars.

What do you think you'll learn from managing your money this way?

Glossary

barrel race: A race in which a horse and rider race around three barrels set up in a cloverleaf pattern.

bay: A dark reddish-brown horse with a black mane and tail.

broom polo: A game played on horseback with brooms instead of polo mallets, and a large rubber ball.

chestnut: A reddish-colored horse with either a red or lighter colored mane and tail.

cinch: The strap that holds the saddle in place.

dressage: The art of ballet-like movements made by the horse with a rider.

English pleasure: European-style riding class at a horse show; saddles are smaller and do not have a saddle horn.

fitting and showing: The lead line class at a horse show in which the horse is judged on cleanliness, condition, and handling.

flag race: This is when a horse and rider race individually to pick up a flag at one end of the arena, then deposit it at the other end.

gelding: A male horse that has been castrated.

half pass: A high level dressage movement in which the horse moves gracefully on the diagonal, legs crossing over at each step.

lead line class: This is when a handler leads the horse instead of riding.

palomino: A golden-colored horse with a white mane and tail.

passage: The high level dressage movement in which the horse trots in slow motion.

pinto: A flashy colored horse with black and white patches.

pole bending: A type of individual horseback race in which the horses weave in and out of closely spaced poles as fast as possible.

vaulting: This skill is displayed when a rider performs gymnastics on horseback while the horse canters in a small circle.

western pleasure: The riding class at a horse show in which the horse is judged on smoothness and obedience, and the tack is "cowboy style" (saddle with a horn).

Annette Johnston is a financial advisor by day, which supports her many hobbies and interests. She is also the proud owner of Frolic Farm, where her many furry, feathered, and finned friends live. You can meet her critters online at www.frolicfarm.com.

Annette has "horsed around" with many wonderful horses over the years which have provided the inspiration for this book. Annette also enjoys woolly crafts such as knitting and felting projects with wool from her own sheep.

In her free time, Annette performs Baroque music on her soprano recorder in duets with the organ/harpsichord. She has two successful CDs of her classical music that she sells to support various charities.

Please visit Annette at

www.frolicfarm.com